Some Sunny Day

Some Sunny Day

Paul Davies

INSOMNIAC PRESS

The setting, characters, and circumstance of this novel are fictional,
even as real or historical persons, places, or events might be described.
Thanks to Mike O'Connor, Philip Leon, Bill Keith,
Simon Dardick, Joan Francuz, and Jack David.

CANADIAN CATALOGUING IN PUBLICATION DATA
Davies, Paul, 1954-
Some sunny day / Paul Davies.
ISBN 1-894663-95-0
1. Title.
PS8557.A8197S64 2005   C813 .54   C2005-903425-4

The publisher gratefully acknowledges the support of the Canada
Council, the Ontario Arts Council and the Department of Canadian
Heritage through the Book Publishing Industry Development Program.

Printed and bound in Canada.

Insomniac Press
192 Spadina Avenue, Suite 403,
Toronto, Ontario, Canada M5T 2C2
www.insomniacpress.com

We'll meet again,
Don't know where,
Don't know when,
But I know we'll meet again,
Some sunny day.

PARKER and CHARLES, *We'll Meet Again*

Once I was a soldier,
And I fought on foreign sands for you.
Once I was a hunter,
And I brought home fresh meat for you.
Once I was a lover,
And I searched behind your eyes for you.

TIM BUCKLEY, *Once I Was*

for Sherab Drolma
whose story this is

།ཕྱུག་འཚལ་བདེ་མ་དགེ་མ་ཞི་མ།
།བདག་གི་ཚེ་རབས་སྟོན་ནས་བསྐྱབས་པའི་ལྷ།
།སྐྱ་ངན་འདས་ཞི་སྐྱིད་ཡུལ་ཉིད་མ།།

When he first came into the store I could see he was taken with me.

People were frequently taken with me because I was young and attractive. Slender and full-breasted, with a knock-'em-dead smile. A sexy white smile that could slay the sourest heart.

I'm not boasting, saying that plainly now. Even when I thought well of myself at the time, I didn't have the confidence to tell anyone, and was often confused about the value of these gifts to me as a person.

If you roll your eyes at this matter of the person inside, you are already lost to yourself and have no business reading my diary any further. Goodbye.

I could have shunned my own attractiveness and let it fall into ruin. But I didn't.

I didn't play it up particularly either. I was an active person, and the activity of my life kept me fit. I watched what I ate, a vegetarian diet mostly, and cared about my health and hygiene. I dressed well, admittedly often in tight-fitting things to accent my shape, but without any special urge to be fashionable or seductive.

Why shouldn't I enjoy the face and body I'd been blessed with? Most of the time, it made me happy about myself. Besides, beauty might be slandered as fleeting and fickle, but make no mistake — it has great value while it lasts.

It also has limitations to reconcile, of course, and contradictions. You learn that it brings you undeserved opportunities. You learn how it can forgive other inadequacies. You learn that its power is not absolute.

Ugliness, instead, is usually tragic for the person inside, but wields little power and is less complex.

Although, standards for both are different in different places and have changed over time. For instance, the way Titian liked chubby girls. That sort of thing.

My body had appeal in my own time and place.

Excessive appeal at times, and I'd learned at an early age that I had to defend myself against exploitation.

As a young adult, I could decide for myself whether an action was exploitation or pleasure. Decisions I made for myself didn't have to be consistent either. I could take risks, and experiment. I suffered for my bad decisions and enjoyed some deliberate excesses. Whatever I did, I tried to be true to myself and to avoid situations I could see would be hurtful. I was wounded from time to time, when I couldn't see.

There was something about this person — the man taken with me that day in the store — that didn't fit the usual pattern.

Looking into his eyes, I felt peaceful.

Looking into mine, he was paralyzed.

I'd had lots of guys go apeshit seeing me for the first time, but never before a seizure quite like this. His jaw dropped to the floor and his face went white. He couldn't move a muscle.

I was fearful for a moment. Anyone at all can come into a retail store, and we got as many nutbars as any other place.

But this wasn't a nutbar. I could tell by the softness in his eyes.

And it wasn't sexual. Wasn't desire. This I could spot blindfolded and locked in the trunk of a car, being frequently pursued.

He muttered a few syllables, unintelligible, collecting himself.

Then he said, "Are you a dancer?"

I smiled. The famous smile, although it didn't deepen his distress. That was already past saturation.

"No," I said.

"Oh," he replied.

The colour was gone from his cheeks. Like someone in shock, I thought.

I liked that. I liked him. The greater part of me had assumed an attitude of defense — I always did that speaking with someone for the first time — but I still liked him. Whatever had disarmed him seemed to me innocent, even sweet.

"You are the living likeness of someone I knew once," he said. "A dancer. She was a dancer. I didn't think you were she. But I wondered if you might be a dancer too. Just that you might be."

8

He was trying to recover. I didn't punish him.

"No, I've never done anything like that."

Another smile.

I could see his body was beginning to relax a little.

"What's your name?"

"Laura."

"Her name was Gabrielle. My friend the dancer, I mean. I didn't think you were her. That was quite a few years ago. But I thought you might be one yourself. Just having a dancer's body."

"Nope," I said.

"A remarkable likeness."

I smiled again. He smelled nice, too. Although I could tell he smoked.

"Please forgive my behaving like this," he said, gradually coming to grips with himself. "I was just amazed at the likeness."

"That's nice," I said blithely.

He glanced down, and my gold bracelet caught his eye. Then he looked at my hands, rotating his head slightly.

"You've written 'Big Nose' on the back of your hand," he quietly observed. "What does that mean?"

A slight startle came to his face. He'd pulled himself out of one danger only to plunge headlong into another.

"If you don't mind my asking," he added.

I occasionally wrote reminders to myself on the back of my hand with a ballpoint pen, if there was no paper handy, but I couldn't remember what I was thinking when I wrote this!

"I don't know!" I said, and laughed.

I didn't know if I should trust him. I thought he was sweet, but I was cautious toward him, at first.

Now I know the weight he was bearing inside. I would have done worse than he, had things been reversed. Had it been me who'd remembered, seeing him suddenly. Had it been me who'd been looking.

Looking — and hoping. Every day for twenty years, getting up every morning, hopeful. Then, much later along, finally giving up. Or, if not giving up, adjusting.

Then suddenly, unexpectedly, seeing her. Knowing it is her. Knowing.

"Um, maybe we could go for coffee sometime," he said.

"I only drink tea," I said.

"Gabrielle only drank tea," he answered.

2002

I

I've been lying here for a while. This isn't my usual bed.

I'm not sure where I am.

Except that I've passed on and come to a strange place. A place that seems like where I was before — the world where I was before — but far away, and in a different time.

I read a novella once about a girl who suddenly found herself in a different place and time, as a ghost in the ancient world. It was a good story.

But that isn't my story. I haven't been swept into adventure. I am dead. I was living out a happy, prosperous, flesh-and-blood career on the western side of planet Earth at the start of the twenty-first century and now that life is over.

My brilliant career.

It was that.

I say it that way from a book title. *My Brilliant Career* was the fictional memoir of a young woman who travelled to Australia in the nineteenth century, weathering her way through much hardship. Miles Franklin, its author, lived that life on a grazing property in New South Wales, publishing her book in 1901. It was made into a movie in 1979, at the end of which the heroine was shown bundling up her fat manuscript in brown paper and tying it with string, then dropping the parcel in a pick-up box at the end of a dusty desert road in the Australian outback. Her only copy, hand-written, addressed to a publisher in Edinburgh, eleven thousand miles and months and months away by sea.

I found a pen and paper here, so I thought I should keep a diary. Of this present transformation, my uncertain career. To be sure I remember everything, and to look back at in case I get confused.

I'm not confused now. I don't fully understand my situation, but that doesn't mean I'm confused.

My aunt worked at the University of Toronto in the 60s, and told me how one day she was getting her mail in the department office when the secretary came in, amused that Marshall McLuhan had left a note on her windscreen. "You are parked in my spot," it said, signed "Marshall." When Professor McLuhan himself arrived, the secretary leapt up and gleefully said, "Marshall! This is the first time you've written something I could understand!"

No one has left me a note offering a simple explanation. But, what I'm supposed to do will be clear to me soon, I think. For the moment, though, I'm heartsick. Stalled with a knotted, aching feeling in my chest. They left me here to rest and collect myself.

I've done that, but my mind often wanders.

Earlier I imagined myself to be like the person in Kafka's tale who discovers he's changed into a beetle. Although the meaning of this in Kafka isn't about heartache, I don't think, but has to do with loss of identity or some other inner oppression.

I read that Kafka story a long time ago, in school. I went through quite a few books in school but wasn't a big reader after that.

Except the morning newspaper, and magazines.

I'd often pick up magazines at the newsstand if I took an interest in something. There are good ones about woodworking, which I liked. And geography. Also about health and fitness, and yoga. And gardening. Fashion. Geography. Just about everything under the sun. And astronomy magazines, for things not under the sun.

Those about astronomy were strewn with advertisements for telescopes and related paraphernalia. I bought them because I began to wonder what was up in the night sky. I knew it was the moon and stars and all, but I didn't understand what I was seeing.

One day I saw a magazine cover that promised to explain what stars were, how far away they were, and about their heat and size and light. I was curious and bought it.

I wasn't always curious like that. Most of the time, though at different times, I was mainly concerned with men, or having money to spend, or gaining others' esteem of me. But as time went on those things got easier and didn't hold my interest like they had before.

I might've been curious about death, but it didn't come to mind very often. I once suggested to a friend in Vancouver that he write a Canadian Book of the Dead; like the Tibetan one, except the passage through the Bardo was along East 41st Avenue, and its stages were the span of Vancouver streets named for trees. I loved those street names. Balsam. Elm. Larch. Yew. Laurel. Ash. Cypress.

Oh boy. I'm rambling.

Sorry about that.

I've been lying here for quite a while now.

"Here" meaning in a small basement room. "Lying" meaning half-naked on an old duvet covering an iron-framed single bed. There's a mirror and sink opposite, on the wall. High up on one side of that, a tiny window draped with a tattered white sheer.

The ceiling plaster is cracked and fallen away. I've been studying it. I think people often do that when they've been lying in bed a long time.

There's a toilet in a little closet beside the sink, but I haven't had to use it. I haven't eaten either, but I've not felt hungry. Something has changed. My body seems both in the world and not.

I don't mind the part about not eating. One of the major horrors of life is that living things have to eat other living things to survive.

I haven't tried to escape since being left here. I don't know if I can or not. But I'm not under any threat, and don't want to be out of the frying pan and into the fire. I've imagined myself going outside and suddenly entering some hellish place, then returning to find the door locked behind me.

That happened to me once when I lived downtown. I had an attic room with a shared bath and was down the hall one morning drying off after my shower when I heard the door to my room blow shut. Wham! Well, I had to climb out my neighbour's window in my underwear and crawl across the flashing edge into my window from the outside. I made it safely, but a scissor-sharpening man on the street below raised a great commotion. He was peeling an orange with a pen-knife as he ambled by, pulling his foot-treadle sharpening cart. He happened to see me up there, trembling in my underwear straddling the two windows, and started ringing his big brass bell and shouting "Bandit! Bandit!" in a loud voice. Holy shit. Really added colour to the ordeal, I'll tell you.

I always call myself a "girl" rather than a "woman," by the way. It's just an expression — a kind of self-endearment — that I say when I'm thinking. When I talk to myself. It comes from Catullus, the Roman poet, whom I read in school.

Vale, puella! *Goodbye, girl!*

I've been talking to myself this morning, about feeling so heart-sick. About metaphysics.

I say that knowing what the word means. I read a Bertrand Russell paperback about metaphysics in school, and he said it meant "comprehending the universe by means of thought."

So I've been lying in bed, disconsolate, comprehending the universe by means of thought. Trying to, anyway.

I've said a lot about my aching inside. You're alone in death in the most intensive way, you see. Like if you'd had a trauma, or been angry, and you phone and write your friends for comfort, but nobody writes back. Nobody returns your call.

2

When I tell you how I found myself in this place, and what I've remembered since, I don't think you'll find it very probable. But it might be interesting, or at least entertaining.

We might agree to call it a dream. People can accept any kind of fantastic tale if you say it was a dream. Dream scenarios don't have the same moment as fact for people, of course. But, then again, lots of believable stories you've heard from people have almost certainly been complete bullshit, whereas my unlikely tale is true.

Let's still agree to call it a dream. The passage after death is a lot like dreaming.

I'm not saying I know very much about dreams. I don't think anyone does. Ambiguous, perhaps, the "unconscious" being such a big part of ourselves; but that's just how it is.

In life, that is. I'm less clear about all of that now, in death.

But I do exist.

I was full of regret earlier that I'd lost my life at such a young age. I was only twenty-seven. But I realized I was feeling that regret, and it went away. My life was over, but my essence had remained intact. Moreover, this essence was aware of itself, and of its presence, and had thoughts. Feeling regret over my own death was immediate proof of that.

At bottom, that's all people really wonder about death — if they exist afterwards. Oh, there's lots of whys and wherefores, but I think their own continuity is the only thing people are trying to reconcile with questions about death.

You may think this an interesting opportunity, to read the diary of someone who has already gone. It will probably come as a huge assurance that I still exist to write it; but in some other respects you'll probably be disappointed.

You see, I cannot tell you any more about the objective truths of death than you can tell me about the objective truths of life.

You say, "Why not! You are there!" and I make the same reply to you, "Why not, you are there!" It's staring you in the face, and you don't know what it is.

So, yes, death surrounds me like a deep warm ocean, and I am no more certain of what it is, and what I am in it, than you are of your life and what you are in that.

I could still give it a shot.

Death is existence, experience, recollection, restitution, and reflexion.

Sounds a lot like life you say.

Yes, for me it has been. Except you don't seem to add anything to what you came with. Seems that dynamic is an exclusive quality of life.

Regardless, I cannot offer any assurance about what'll happen to you in death.

This is why I warned you earlier you'd be disappointed.

I'm sitting here writing a death diary. You, on the other hand, might find yourself at the right hand of the Lamb of God, expired into the silent void, or selling subway tickets in Manhattan. I don't know what, and I don't know why, even though I'm here.

You'll also be disappointed that I arrived here with a problem. One might hope and expect to find peace and rest in death, but I've found wondering and apprehension instead.

I've learned that I'm part-way through a journey of discovery. I have recovered its genesis, from which visions I now rest.

I'd like to have another go at those visions, with more refined questions in mind. But I know I won't get the chance.

That also sounds a lot like life, doesn't it? The way someone at fifty so often wants to repossess themselves at twenty-five, bringing along all they've learned since.

But it just doesn't work that way, of course. Unless you're a perfected yogi, in which case it no longer matters.

You might think that death would be bigger than life in this, but it's not. I only got answers to the questions I asked. If you ask small questions, you'll get small answers. The depth of your questions in death is a thing cultivated in life.

Which brings to mind the best advice I can give, whether you seek the void, heavenly fields, union with Christ Jesus, absolution in nature, or whatever else.

That advice is: *This is it*. Your experiences and their outcomes are the logical consequences of your own nature.

You've heard it before.

All this said, I'm not disappointed with the knowledge I gained from my long panorama. Not in itself. My questions were about my journey, and the answers were what I wanted to know.

I only wish I'd been thinking about a broad range of concerns, instead of mainly about love, when I first entered into it.

Oh well.

One could do worse than focus on love.

I just need some more thought to work out what I'm supposed to do next. What I've seen was singularly pertinent to my journey, so I know the essential clue is there.

Oh — I've just remembered something from an astronomy magazine I read once, which urges me to caution you in another respect. It was a photograph from the Hubble space telescope, of two galaxies in collision.

I was looking at the photo in the magazine, and behind the two big galaxies in collision I noticed some tiny objects. Like star-points; but looking more closely I saw they were crisp little spirals. Whole galaxies! Some face-on, others more oblique. A dozen or more! Each a billion stars. All of them in a mere pinpoint of light, not visible to the largest telescopes on the planet surface.

Looking at that photo, it occurred to me we are quite solipsistic in our thinking on this planet.

I won't say more about these things. But I thought you'd find it odd if I didn't say anything at all. Some parts — about death — may have sounded a little forced. This is because questions about death are only asked by the living. I'm already dead. The questions I've had since dying have been about life.

I wish Leonard Cohen was here. He'd know what to do. Or, if he didn't, he'd still bring his heartwarming smile, and a song.

I think I should go soon. It appears they aren't coming back to get me but have left me here for a rest, after which I must go of my own impulse.

Before I do, I'll tell you about my arrival here. It might be interesting for you, or at least entertaining.

3

I was run down by a van. A delivery van. I'd been to see a musical at one of the theatres downtown. I was walking back to the car park after the show when it happened. The van was bringing gifts of flowers from well-wishers to the stage door. I was wearing a gown. A pretty gown, in the colours of a Cornish war tartan. My family was Cornish.

I was dazed after getting hit. In shock. I could see the impact coming, and my mind instantly filled with a panicked appeal to Superman, to swoop down out of the sky and save the day.

Can you remember a time you've been panicked? A person does not spare much time for orderly thought. I didn't anyway. I wasn't thinking about whether or not I was going to die, or wondering what would happen to me if I did.

I can tell you this as well. Your earthly career doesn't flash before your eyes before you go. Or, maybe it has for others, but it didn't for me. I just felt distraught and paralyzed and helpless, together with that vague-but-urgent wish that something — like the Man of Steel — would swoop down and rescue me.

When I woke up, I didn't remember anything about flower vans, or where I was, or who I'd been. It was dark, and I was flustered. I could remember something about tartan, though, because I noticed I was wearing a skirt of that fabric. But it wasn't yellow-green. It was in tones of grey, like striped charcoal. My blouse was also grey. I was lying down, curled up on hard, black earth.

Asphalt. I realized it was asphalt. More tar than you'd find in the asphalt on a Toronto street, though. Gummy asphalt, with the strangely sentimental aroma of a hot smudge-pot.

I didn't know where I was, or what I was doing, but I knew I was dead.

For a moment I was excited. The excitement of discovery — once having determined I wasn't injured, or in any apparent danger. As I got to my feet, I felt strangely fit.

What I saw there was disappointing. Standing on the tarmac, I could see irregular squat hills and peaks all around me. As though I was in a heavenly valley. Only paved over.

The sun was just coming up, and the fresh light revealed the hills to be heaps of scrap metal. The stubby summits weren't made of rock and snow and trees, but rather of twisted iron and steel and copper and brass. The heap ahead of me looked like the cut-up remains of a freighter. Broad sheets of formed iron, piled high, many still with the lines and figure of a ship, dimpled with giant rivets. Behind me, another sizable mound, mostly of copper pipe and fittings, punctuated with an assortment of bronze castings here and there. The refuse of a thousand demolished bathrooms. Just to the other side, a smaller pile. Old auto parts mostly. Vintage parts. Colourful curly fenders and bulbous headlamps and things you'd only see on priceless antiques.

I stood there staring around me for an hour or more.

It's hard to explain why I didn't start walking. I just didn't feel any urge to move.

As the sun broke into full morning daylight, I noticed a small, spindly, mobile steam crane away down the main asphalt path, with its broad shiny jaws collapsed on the ground at the end of two pairs of twisted steel cables.

To one side of the copper heap, past a clamour of spoked wheels and hubs, I saw there were walls. Tall walls made of wooden planks, painted brown and yellow, maybe twelve feet high, all around the place. Walling in about a half-acre of scrap.

It was a junkyard.

I laughed.

"Doesn't appear I've gone to heaven," I said dryly.

"Aye, ye 'ave surely not!" I heard a voice say from behind me.

I was startled and turned to face the most extraordinary man. I could hardly believe my eyes. He was half constructed of metal, like he'd ransacked his own junkyard for body parts. One full mechanical leg on his right side, the apparatus connecting around his backside and down his thigh as a brace for the leg on his left. I couldn't help but stare.

"Ne'er seen a cripple b'fore?" he asked tersely.

"No, sir!" I blurted out. "I mean — *Yes*, sir." And gave a little smile. I didn't mean to antagonize him.

"I was admiring the workmanship."

That was true, and I think he believed me. But it wasn't what I'd ever expect — nothing resembling the clinical steel contraptions I'd seen before. Instead, it was made of rosettes of tarnished brass, shaped to the contours of a human leg and connected in an intricate weave with tiny rivets. Like fine metal crochet, precisely articulated at the knee and ankle.

"Aye, the forge and smith's been my skill o'er many a year," he said, giving me a fresh start as I noticed one of his hands was also mechanical, finely shaped and jointed, made of the same intricate brasswork — and so was the top of his head! That part wasn't functional, though. It was a kind of hat he wore. A helmet.

The pant-leg above the metal limb was torn short at the thigh, the brace supporting his other leg obvious beneath his trousers. Otherwise he was attired as I'd imagine any yardman might be. A loose-fitting cotton shirt and a long white overcoat in straight conservative lines, tailored in a lightweight fabric below a small square collar. Quite soiled, though, to put it kindly.

Being fascinated with his various mechanical fittings, I took in his facial features last.

When I finally did, I was filled with dread. The man's face was menacing just to look at. A threatening, sinister leer was built in. If that wasn't enough, he'd gone on to garnish its landscape with an assortment of scars from various cuts, scrapes, and burns over the years. Centuries, it looked like.

"A hazardous skill it be," he said, as though he could read my mind, which only added to my apprehension of him.

As he said that, a bone-man appeared from between the mountains of metal, pulling a loaded cart along the asphalt toward us. He rested it a few feet from where we stood and walked up nearly nose-to-ear with me.

He was younger and better kept than metal-man, also wearing a cotton overcoat, well-worn and stained. He seemed to have his own body parts, at least. Standing together, they looked like a pair of unhappy cricket referees, who'd maybe found themselves pitched off a moving bus into a drainage ditch.

"Conversin' with the one ye love best, are ye Festus?" the man said to him.

"Aye, that be so," Festus replied, his voice dropping, then turned to look at me severely. "Cae ye see any other about?!"

"None but thee!" the bone-man said, and snorted.

I wasn't sure what was so funny, but a chill came over me as I realized he was telling the truth. I was completely invisible to him.

Festus offered him three shillings and ha'penny for the weight of lead and tin he'd pulled in on his cart. Done on a handshake, Festus fetched the money and sent him on his way.

The currency on offer gave me a good idea of what country I was in, for a start at orienting myself. Coming back to where I stood waiting, Festus looked me all up and down.

"What spectre may ye be, my man of the grey tartan? Now say it clearly, and know ye 'ave no power o'er me, whate'er ye be."

"I don't know!" I appealed with a sudden wave of arms and hands. "Um . . . I don't know, except I'm not your 'man' of the grey tartan. I'm your 'woman'."

He seemed only mildly surprised, stepping back to sum up my body in a second single, slow, head-to-toe glance.

"I just found myself here. A few hours before you showed up." I paused before adding, "I don't think I'm alive anymore. I mean, I know I'm here talking to you, but this isn't my life anymore. I don't think it is."

I wasn't worried Festus would dismiss me as a nut if I spoke plainly like that. He'd called me a "spectre," and he knew his bone-man couldn't see me. He'd asked him outright, although the man was unaware of what was under test on the instant.

"Aye," Festus said, screwing up one side of his face. "Aye."

Alive or dead, I was apparently in the same world as he because the next thing I knew he'd taken firm hold of a wad of fabric at my breast with all five fingers of his good hand.

"We'll soon sort ye out!" he shouted, pulling me along by the blouse pocket toward one end of the junkyard. He put his mech-anical hand to his lips and whistled loudly, but no one answered.

Coming around the dismantled freighter, I could see the far end of the yard was actually the back wall of a large brick structure. The yellow junkyard fence joined the building snug to the stone at either corner. I had the sense there was a busy street to the farther side, in front of the place. I couldn't see anything, but there were the sounds of urban goings-on over the way.

The back of the building on the junkyard side had one entry, a large steel door to the extreme left as we approached, standing at ground level above a shallow concrete porch. A bell-shaped metal lampshade, absent of a bulb, hung out over the porch at the end of a long skinny curl of tubing fastened into the wall above the door frame. Rising to one side of that, nearly to the peak of the roof four-and-a-half stories above, was a wooden fire escape with a small navy-blue door at each landing. Not only in good repair, but nicely made and painted flat white. Festus must've had a talent for carpentry too, I thought.

The bricks and mortar up the back of the building were also well maintained, if darkened with age and soot. There were only two small windows on the whole back face, to either side on the second floor, their frames nicely painted to match the fire escape doors. I could see they were curtained behind.

The ornamental gables and drainage troughs were painted the same blue, the roof itself some kind of dark slate or ceramic tile. Attached to the fire escape facing at the third level was a colourful sign: *The Asphodel Music Hall*.

How interesting! I said to myself. A vaudeville theatre. A big brown-brick burlesque palace.

"I'll come with you freely," I appealed to Festus with a flimsy smile as we briskly, but rhythmically, clanked along to the sound of his various brass fittings.

"Okay, then," he said with a grunt, letting go of my blouse, but putting his hand behind my upper arm instead. Just to be sure I kept up the pace.

When we got to the back door, he pulled a ring of keys up from his belt, like you might see on a gaoler in the cartoon strips. He jangled them around — skeleton keys, which I couldn't tell one from another — until finding the one he knew would turn the lock.

Which it did, grinding and chiming around one full turn with the crisp precision of a well-adjusted mechanical cash register.

He grabbed my shirt again, pulling me through the broad doorway and along a corridor, cluttered with the trappings of a theatre back entrance. Whitewashed plaster walls, with colourful burlesque posters and announcements tacked up here and there, and a security kiosk a short way along.

We stopped there momently, gazing through the reception win-dow, a three-foot-high pane of glass flush in a narrow wood frame, commencing at waist level. It had a hole to speak through, like the ticket window at a movie theatre. There were three women sitting in the office behind, each wearing metallic bandeaux with silk tap pants and sleazy fishnet stockings, to whom Festus waved. They glanced up at him but made no gesture in return. I could hear trum-pet players warming up, and an organ, or calliope, from somewhere not far away. And the clicking of heels and toes, like tap dancers.

We quickly came to the end of the corridor, which turned sharply into a much broader hallway — the back foyer. I was struck by how suddenly the scenery was transformed. The ceiling leapt up to eighteen or twenty feet overhead, the whitewash giving way to beautiful wood paneling. Dark, like teak or mahogany, with wooden ribs forming panels, each about four feet square, stacked up to the ceiling down both facing walls. Fastened into an ornamental tin ceiling overhead were four small crystal chandeliers, spaced at regular intervals, each with three electric lightbulbs. Here and there ahead of me I could see slatted shipping crates piled on the tile floor, spilling straw packing material and draped over with ropes or broad stretches of cloth. About midway down the foyer on the far side there was a short, broad stair.

Pulled along by the shirt again I could briefly see as we passed that this led up to the backstage area and dressing rooms.

There was a drunk asleep there as we went by, sprawled on the steps snoring open-mouthed, his face and hands stained with claret, apparently late of a bottle stuffed in his jacket pocket.

"He be the supreme ruler of heaven and earth," Festus said.

"Sure he is," I said under my breath, with the gentlest involun-tary roll of my eyes.

There were four doors along the wall opposite the backstage stair. Entering to offices, or small rehearsal studios, I thought.

One of the doorways, lit by the chandelier farthest down the foyer from the entranceway, led to the basement — a discovery I made when Festus opened it with a firm twist of its shiny brass doorknob and escorted us both down the stair.

Entering the basement, the handsome wooden decor of the foyer gave way to something on the barbarous side of rustic. The rough stair descended at a precipitous grade, swaying and creaking under our weight as we descended its twenty-odd steps, with only the questionable comfort of a skinny handrail on one side. The cellar walls were of rough stone and earth, with a piquant musty smell and clinging traces of spiderwebs.

The air improved slightly as we crossed the hollow at the foot of the stair, passing into gloom. Festus struck a flint installed in the thumb of his mechanical hand, igniting a wick in the adjacent brass forefinger to light our way. By the flicker of this peculiar candle I could see we'd entered a dungeon of fat wooden pillars supporting thick joists beneath numerous rows of ceiling beams about ten feet overhead. We proceeded across the stone floor toward what would be the street-side of the theatre above. As we walked, I noticed a large steam boiler and other plumbing off to one side of us, and the dusty cables and switches of a crude electrical system to the other. Several yards ahead there was another doorway, the only passage through a load-bearing wall of thick stone standing the full beam of the cellar.

Festus pulled the door open and led me through, where, past the extreme breadth of the wall, we came into a spacious room. I glanced up as I entered, picturing myself under row upon row of theatre seats fastened into the top side of the ceiling beams — the floor of the music hall above.

I had a start as I turned to inspect the chamber. I thought it must be a conference of the dead! Ghostly forms in murky white, large and small, strewn all about.

Unfortunately, there was an eerie logic to that. I *was* dead, after all. I wondered if he'd brought me there to attend a conference of my peers.

They proved to be dusty white sheets draped over an assortment of old furnishings. There were two electric bulbs above, each dangling bare at the end of a foot of twisted wire. Festus lit them both with the snap of a switch on the wall, snuffing his fingertip torch against his leather belt as he did so.

He pulled away one of the sheets, revealing a chair. A throne, more like. It was fantastic! Kind of a white-streaked grey-green marble, with its arms carved in the shape of dolphins, and other decorations inlaid in gold and mother-of-pearl. It must have been built for one of their vaudeville shows, I reasoned. At the same time, it seemed too striking for that. Too opulent. The seat cushion was sealskin, I think.

"Ye be sat there, and be put to the place," Festus said firmly. "And be of respect," he added. "This be the chair of Poseidon, Lord of the Seas and Oceans, who be gone from us now."

"Sure thing," I said, wondering what he meant by that. He did not seem to be joking!

"I'll return to ye with another who'll sort the matter out."

What that meant I could not know: whether a questioning, beating, or slaughter. Though I didn't have much to lose. I was already dead, of course.

I pinched myself to see if I could feel pain — to see how I might react if I had hours of grisly physical torture in store. My spirits declined slightly as I found I felt the prick of my fingernails well enough.

But I just sat quietly, trying to keep calm, admiring the throne. The marble positively hummed with its own smooth, lustrous elegance. The more I looked at it — even in the dim light of the two bare light bulbs — the more entranced I became. It was of such exceptional polish, to the eye it seemed of infinite depth, as though you'd be just as likely to sink right into it, or pass clear through, as sit against firm stone.

I could see there were a number of big chairs there, among other items, all covered with white sheets. I could tell by the shape of several that they were thrones too. Though I didn't dare get up and look. My head was clear, but I wasn't sure what was happening to me exactly, and the last thing I wanted to do was get into trouble with the only person (soon to be persons) that I'd happened to make contact with.

After a time — maybe ten minutes, or a little longer — Festus returned with a woman.

Wow! I was amazed!

She was over six feet tall, and radiant of a physical strength that would have humbled a champion prizefighter. Not beautiful, exactly; but very handsome, and assuredly feminine. Cool, strong features. Long shiny black hair. Firm olive-coloured skin. She was wearing a matched vest and skirt of smooth leather, ivory-yellow in colour, like natural pigskin.

Festus was calling her "dearest"; but frankly, I couldn't imagine a strong, handsome, smooth-skinned Amazon like her loaning a bus ticket to an eroded fossil like Festus.

She didn't reply to him, but then again, she wasn't saying much of anything. So I didn't know if she was ignoring his affections or if she was usually silent.

I stood up when she came into the room, as a courtesy, but with a gesture of her hand she instructed me to sit again.

She stared at me, walking first to one side, then to the other, a look of concentration on her face. At one point she waved for me to get to my feet, then to turn around, all the while examining me intently with her eyes.

Beautiful eyes, too. Dark, clear eyes.

"What is your name?" she asked at length.

"Laura!" I said, having only remembered it that very second.

"Laura," she repeated flatly. This wasn't a preface to anything. She was just trying it on her tongue.

"Why did you come to this place, Laura?" she asked me after another minute or so.

"Why?" I asked in return. "I don't know! I don't know what or where 'this place' is."

"I see," she replied.

Festus was starting to fidget. He'd been standing quietly off to one side, favouring his one flesh-and-blood foot, while the woman conducted her inspection of me. She suggested he get back out to the junkyard, that she'd be fine alone with me now.

She had no worries on my account. It was clear she could squash any revolt from me with little effort.

Festus nodded and went on his way.

25

The woman sat down facing me in another of the big chairs, without removing its cover sheet. After a few minutes she spoke.

"Do you know who we are?" she asked.

"I know nothing," I said.

She kept me in suspense through another long pause.

She might have been hypnotizing me with her gaze, because I began to remember things. In particular, I suddenly recovered the details of my death.

"I've just remembered something!" I blurted out.

"Yes," she said coolly.

"I'm dead!" I said, with a relish that seemed strange to me even as I said it. "I was hit by a flower truck."

She nodded.

"Outside of a theatre," I said. "A concert hall."

"What concert had you seen?" she asked.

"A musical — that is, I mean, an opera — *Orphée et Eurydice*," I responded clumsily.

The woman got to her feet and came over and leaned into my face, supporting her outstretched hands on the fat dolphin heads.

"You must have been listening to that opera with religious fer-vour," she said.

"What?" I answered blandly.

"You have come to purgatory."

My mind went blank.

"A purgatory that no one attends anymore."

"What do you mean?"

"You have entered a purgatory that has been barren of human souls for seventeen centuries."

"Oh," I said.

"We do not want you here," the woman said.

"I'll go then!" I blurted out, not knowing what I was saying.

"You cannot leave," she replied.

"Well, one hates to be an unwelcome guest," I said, and let out a nervous laugh.

"You *are* an unwelcome guest," she answered, and sat back down on her shrouded throne.

She was silent for several minutes. I began a careful inspection of the ceiling to avoid her scrutiny.

"Purgatory is an intermediate world," she said at last. "A place where your unresolved crimes are requited."

"Yes, I know that," I answered.

"And you know you have crimes?" she asked flatly.

"I suppose I must," I said. "But I don't know what they are. I didn't murder anyone or steal anything. Nothing like that."

She fell silent again, avoiding my gaze this time. I was suddenly a little impatient for her to get to the point.

"No one comes to this purgatory anymore. We are long forgotten to men. Those of us gathered here are only recently together again, after many centuries apart. Several others are lost to us still. Some are lost to us forever."

"After many centuries?" I interrupted.

There was a sudden compelling sadness in her voice.

"For millennia we together were sovereign of the earth, sky, seas, and underworld. We reigned supreme, and then — after a time so lengthy it seemed everlasting — it was over. One morning the sun rose in the sky, and it was over."

"When was that?" I asked meekly, already anticipating the full drift of her story.

"After Julian of Constantinople came to power, in the fifth century of the common era. The morning of that woesome day the sister Fates announced we must destroy all evidence of ourselves and our domains and vanish. We were exiled, an ignominious destiny after our devoted service to the earth, and the reverence of man — after reigning supreme over man. Now the humility of poverty and anonymity has reigned on us each day for fifteen centuries."

She paused, then continued.

"Only twenty survived in exile that we have located. Thirty years ago, one among us made an exceptional effort to bring us together again, to this place. She had the help of a soul of ancient Mycenae, who still wanders the netherworld of your purgatory."

"But who *are* you?" I pleaded, although I'd pretty much put the pieces together.

It strained my disbelief, though. I needed her to tell me straight out. Of course, my own condition also strained my disbelief. That I was walking and talking as though I were alive, although I knew I was dead. So the idea of her being seven thousand years old didn't seem as incredible that moment as it might have.

"Do you know our names?" she asked me, cocking up one brow.

"The yardman's name is Festus," I said. "I know that."

"We've changed our true names, or at least twisted them about, to disguise them."

"Oh?" I said.

"The yardman's true name is Hephaestus. My name is Athene, although I am here called Amelia."

"Oh!" I said (a little too loudly). "So the guy up by the stage door with the claret must be Zeus!"

That impolite reaction was only because I was suddenly giddy, nervous about what she'd told me. It just seemed so *unlikely* that I'd be face-to-face with someone of legend. She might as well have said that she was Alice, and metal-man was Tweedle-Dee.

I think she must have understood, because she didn't punish me for my rudeness.

"That is correct," was all she said. "He is Zeus."

I wouldn't have felt quite so embarrassed if it'd been Ares or Apollo. But I had to name the right guy *and* have that guy be the big boss. Festus — *Hephaestus* — had said as much when we passed by him, snoring on the stair.

I tried to say something nice, to redeem what I could.

"You were the only one who wasn't intimidated when Odysseus first leapt from directed thought to deciding his life for himself. I always admired that."

She let just a hint of a smile break.

"He was both devoted and fearless," she said.

I hadn't fully recovered my bearing before someone else arrived at the door. She gave Athene a little nod and came in, sitting on the arm of the throne beside her.

This one was really beautiful! The most elegant ancient marble statue you could imagine come to life, with ivory coloured skin, and long dark hair to either side of a thin delicate face. A beautiful face. She was wearing a long dress, plain in style, shaped tight to her body above the waist, flowing in gentle folds below — plain except for a lace top-piece which rose from the bodice above her breasts to a broad lace collar snug around her throat.

"This is Persephone," Athene said.

How appropriate! I thought. The Goddess of the Underworld come to see me. It was flattering in a way.

"What are we going to do with her?" she asked Athene.

"She is here for trial, and will not move on until she has made her restitution."

"But why would she come *here*?"

"She was dreaming the songs of Orpheus when she died."

"Oh, bloody hell," Persephone said, rolling her eyes. Then she looked at me hotly. "We don't have much interest in this sort of thing anymore. Not much interest at all," she said sternly.

"I can see that," I replied.

"Where's the trumpet?" Athene asked aloud, more a declaration than a demand for an answer.

She seemed to have decided what they should do with me, a plan of action unfolding in her mind, which, while unexplained, was apparently now underway.

She *was* the Goddess of Wisdom, and had probably acquired the habit of decisive problem-solving, without much disclosure to others about the plan. After all, none were as judicious and astute as she.

"It must be in this room," Persephone said. Turning to me, she added, "Hestia brought us together here — those that could be found — with the help of a Mycenaean on the other side."

"My side, in purgatory," I said.

"Yes. Being immortals, we can see you there. We have regard to all the earth, oceans, and sky. But no other creature in the sphere of the living will ever see you, nor can they see the Mycenaean."

"His name is Aequitas," Athene said.

"Aequitas?" I blurted out. "How curious that a Greek would call himself by a Latin name!"

29

The word means even-handed, in the sense of providing justice. I remembered that from school.

They didn't answer me.

"Aequitas left Hestia a horn, an Elizabethan sackbut, after we were safely gathered together here. The sound of the horn can be heard only on your side. Aequitas promised its call would summon his return, should we ever need his help again."

So Athene's plan began with mobilizing the assistance of some-one knowledgeable in the ways of my netherworld.

"That was nice of him," I said.

"He has a generous spirit," Athene went on, "with experience of situations like yours."

Persephone had gotten up and was rooting around under the white sheets through various boxes and chests for the instrument — really a trombone, and not a trumpet as Athene called it; a sackbut having a slide, or double slide, depending on how old it was.

Athene joined the search, and it didn't take long for the air to become dark with the dust being thrown up.

"We're only making ourselves grimy this way," Persephone said after a few minutes. "I'll go find Hestia."

Athene tidied up while she was gone, closing trunk lids and replacing their coverings. Then she stood silently by the door.

Persephone returned with Hestia.

She was just how I would've imagined her to be. In late middle age, with a maternal gentleness about her. Her look was mild, and her smile was soft. The Goddess of home and hearth.

She was immediately reassuring.

"You will be on to your long destiny soon," she said warmly.

Then, turning around, she pointed up above the door frame, where a small curl of brass tubing hung in the shadows.

"There it is," she said.

That moment there was an explosion of noise overhead — clari-nets and calliope and voices and feet bursting into music and song and dance.

I was startled by it — though startlings had been a frequent occurrence that morning!

Hestia explained that a rehearsal was getting underway on the stage above. She added that, in addition to their music hall shows — which meant vaudeville comedy, song, dance, and burlesque — they sometimes produced a full-blown musical. It brought in a different class of patron, both expanding their revenue and preserving their standing in the community as having integrity.

"Gilbert and Sullivan," Athene said. "*The Sorcerer*. They're rehearsing the opening now, where everyone comes in dancing and turning cartwheels through the garden."

"I like *The Sorcerer*!" I said — to be friendly, and to show I knew what they were talking about. "I always thought it was underrated, against their other operettas that are more famous. *The Sorcerer*'s got it all — great songs and music, and humour, drama, and mystery as well. Brilliant!"

Persephone looked at me like I was speaking the most tedious few sentences she'd heard in fifty centuries.

"Um . . . you have the horn?" I said sheepishly, trying to quickly change the subject.

Hestia was bringing it down.

"You will have to plug your ears tightly," she said to me. "It is silent to us, being heard by those on your side alone. But the sound to you might be great."

I plugged my ears firmly; but, strangely, that moment I wasn't thinking about the three Goddesses there in front of me, or about my death, or about the Mycenaean they were calling to help me.

My mind drifted. I suddenly felt lonely and helpless. I started to think about the man. The man who came into my store that day, who'd transformed me suddenly in life. There in the cellar of the Gods, deceased, I would never see him again.

Athene put the trombone to her lips and blew. My daydream evaporated as its great brass chorus rumbled through my body, seeming to swell my chest open like a balloon.

A strangely pleasant sensation! The sound was lustrous, far bigger than the small instrument that produced it.

We all stared at each other for a moment, blank-faced, wondering what would happen next.

Which was, over another awkward minute or two, nothing.

"A lot of people wish they were immortal," I said to occupy the pause. Like this time I'd really invested some careful thought to come up with the most banal thing I could possibly say.

"It's hard to keep your interest up," Hestia said kindly, "especially living in obscurity."

"What do you mean?" I asked.

"We've had centuries on our hands with nothing to do!" Persephone said sharply.

"We are no longer moved by achievement or glory, and haven't any of the hope or ambition that spurs men along," Athene added coolly, fulfilling her charge to bring insight to situations.

She had an air of formality about her, both in the way she moved and how she spoke.

The austerity of Godliness, I suppose.

"Over time, the promise of reward in the afterlife gradually became man's principal armour against the pain of living. To the point where life itself — the vibrance of life — paled in favour of that prospect. But we have neither. No reward of life, which has dissolved for us in its own timelessness. Nor the promise of any reward hereafter. We do not die."

"I see," I said.

"Hades stayed behind because of that," Persephone said.

"Stayed behind?"

"In Tartarus," she explained. "He sits alone there still, cold and idle. Alone except for Cerebus. All the others are gone: Charon, the Furies, the judges, and the rest. The energy of the souls once kept there, to all three of its Grounds, faded to nature — vanished to the void of creation — when we fell from power."

"Oh!" I said. "How unfortunate for them!"

Just then a young woman, slender and supple, barely clad in silk stockings and satin dance suit, showed her face at the door.

"This is Thalia, the Grace of the Muses," Hestia graciously informed me in an aside.

I was awestruck yet again. She was just so *sexy*. In life, I think she could have interested me in women!

Whatever it was, seeing one of the Graces, especially the one who was also a Muse, filled me with greater awe than I'd felt for any of the more famous ancient Gods and Goddesses I'd seen that morning.

"There's a big commotion in the junkyard," Thalia said. "You'd better come out before Festus busts his gut completely. Or loses another limb or two."

"Come along!" Athene called to me, as the three of them moved to follow Thalia back up the cellar stair.

She did not try to supervise my progress. I must have given her a quizzical look, because she remarked upon it.

"We only wish you *could* escape, and flee to the distant hills. But you cannot. This theatre and the scrapyard behind are the limit of your universe now — except as you might be escorted away while touching the body or garment of Aequitas, after he arrives."

At least she was clear on the rules and didn't mind telling me what they were.

Zeus was sitting up as we passed the backstage stair. He was talking to a young woman in a burlesque fan-dancer's costume. A revealing one at that, and with plenty worth the revelation.

I hadn't had any sexual interest in women in life, but this was another who could have easily persuaded me. Wow. Almost transcended gender somehow. Just pure heat.

I hope that doesn't sound crude to you, by the way. I've tried to be good-mannered telling you this story.

Hestia waited for me at the top of the basement stair, to walk with me, knowing or expecting that no one else would show me the same consideration.

When we passed the backstage stair I was embarrassed because Hestia had seen the expression on my face, catching a glimpse of the exotic dancer sitting with Zeus.

She just laughed.

"That's her job," Hestia said.

"A stripper?" I asked naïvely.

"She's a dancer now, it's true, but I refer to her role among us in the ancient world."

"You're putting me on," I said flatly. I'd anticipated her.

Hestia laughed a second time.

"I wonder what they might think — if the patrons of this music hall ever knew . . ." I said, fading for a moment, ". . . that the one up on stage, whirling those ostrich plumes around and pulling off her silk underwear, might be . . . No, they'd simply never believe it. They wouldn't know what it meant if they did."

It struck me then how humiliating their lives had become. Just being there — being who they were. It wasn't "how the mighty had fallen" or anything like that. They were the Gods, not baseball players or insurance agents.

Although, please don't ask me to tell you what a God is. As well, I don't want to offend your faith in the God or Gods of your own culture.

After I'd recovered from the pleasant jolt of seeing Aphrodite herself half-naked, we moved quickly along, out of the foyer and down the back-entrance corridor.

The girls that'd been in the reception kiosk when I first arrived were standing outside the back door, open to the junkyard behind.

Hestia must have sensed I was wondering who they were, and whispered that the three were Erato, Euterpe, and Terpsichore: the Muses of erotic poetry, lyric poetry, and dance. Standing there in their stockings and bandeaux, each a little on the chubby side with pretty faces and curly hair. I envied Apollo his wardship.

"Only the four are with us still," Hestia said, meaning the four Muses, including Thalia. "And Apollo, who cares for them," she added, as though knowing my thoughts.

She seemed to have a talent for that. They all did. But, again, they *were* Gods, after all.

Apollo himself was out in the scrapyard, trying to restore order. A good-looking guy, too! Wow!

Hephaestus had lassoed a giant of a man, who I immediately noticed had spooky red eyes like none I'd ever seen before. The hulk was protesting its capture vigorously, pulling and shaking the rope around his enormous arms and chest. All of which was more than a handful for Hephaestus, who'd tied off his end of the lasso to some heavy iron scrap, holding it firmly above the tie-off with his mechanical hand.

Seeing the melée, Hestia was visibly upset.

But it was Persephone who happened to settle matters.

"Festus!" she said with icy authority. "Is this how you treat an honoured guest, whose heart is as ancient as your own? Shame."

That last word had real effect.

Hephaestus instantly released the rope and lowered his head. Sheepishly lifting it a moment later, he appealed that he didn't know who the giant creature was, only that he'd suddenly barged into the junkyard.

"I understand," Persephone said. She only wanted the justice due in the moment, not to create any ill-feeling between them.

Not that they'd all gotten along very well before! Far from it. But their lives and world were different now.

"Hello, Aequitas," Hestia said. "Welcome."

"Welcome, Aequitas," Athene said. "Forgive the reception, if you will."

Aequitas of Mycenae was, obviously, a leviathan. An amber-skinned, seven-foot colossus with ruby-coloured eyes, dressed in light armour — dark leather chest plate, skirt, and shin coverings with brass buckles and fittings — with a large weathered soldier's axe held in his belt.

"Have no concern for it," Aequitas said, with a deep rumbling voice like a streetcar rolling over a track junction.

Even as he exchanged courtesies with the Gods and Goddesses, Aequitas was giving me a hard look-over. He'd turn away when someone spoke to him, then return to me.

Before long he relieved my tension.

"You are a wraith to the living, I observe," he said.

"In purgatory, they said," I answered with a friendly smile. I wanted to be friendly.

Athene explained her understanding of my situation and how I'd arrived there.

"An interesting predicament," Aequitas said. "One I can grasp as natural to the shadow world."

"We should go inside," Persephone said.

"The air is silent here," Aequitas said to Athene.

I didn't know what he meant by that and didn't ask.

Athene knew, however. She explained that, being immortals, they could insulate this place — the boundaries of my purgatory — from the music of the ether. They had greater peace of mind that way, she said.

They didn't take me back down to the basement after we went inside. Even if they'd wanted to, Aequitas could not negotiate the cellar stair, given his size.

Instead, we gathered in a room behind one of the foyer doors opposite the backstage stair, a small rehearsal space. It was painted flat white, with a smooth hardwood floor in a pale finish. There were a number of wooden folding chairs at one end, opposite a fully mirrored wall with a ballet rail. We pulled the chairs into a circle in the middle of the room.

All except Aequitas. He stood.

There was a calendar on the wall beside the door. Printed on the bottom I could see it was compliments of *Southampton Apiary Farms*. Gesturing to it, I asked Athene if this theatre was in Southampton, and she nodded.

The *Titanic* sailed from Southampton.

The page facing was for the month of June 1931. The outdated look of everything suddenly snapped into focus.

I noticed then that Aequitas and I weren't evident in the mirror — the mirrored wall, that is — at all. This would have come as a fresh shock to my comfort, except I was already past that.

I still found it unnerving having no reflexion — and I'd happened to end up sitting facing the mirror in the circle of chairs. So I got up and moved.

"Must be a vampire," Persephone said with a smirk.

"I'll get a mallet and stake," Thalia replied with a big smile, and they all laughed. "Put her out of her misery."

"*Her* misery!" Persephone added, raising another laugh.

That woman was clever, and had a sharp edge to her wit.

"We have to decide what action can be taken," Aequitas said.

"She is here to fulfill some charge upon her," Athene said.

"But what is that charge?" Apollo asked.

"We don't know," Persephone said.

"She could not name any particular crime and has no burden of guilt on any known account," Athene said.

"She's quite a dull person, really," Persephone continued. "Not enough sense to know what she's done, and, whatever it proves to be, it's bound to be trivial."

"That's a relief," I said with some sarcasm. Although she must know a lot about the dead, I thought, having had the job she did in the old world.

"Her deliverance will be through realization," Persephone continued primly, ignoring my remark.

"So how do we get on the trail?" Thalia asked, then added, "I don't mind this at all! Something a little different after hanging around for so long."

"I would rather this were something a little more worthwhile," Persephone said.

"It's true this woman's soul is only one of countless multitudes," Aequitas said. "And that she is ingenuous."

"Ingenious?!" I blurted out.

"That was *ingenuous*," Persephone said. "Innocent and artless."

"Oh," I said. I'm not sure I deserved that assessment, but then I didn't know who or what they might be comparing me with.

Aequitas resumed.

"I have seen so many pass through this sphere. So very many. Some who are wan in spirit, who fade again to the ether. Others sustained by the powerful will of an evil heart. And as many more brimming with beauty and love. I do not know to where any might proceed past this borderland, but I have compassion for all — even for the evil ones among them."

"So we should have pity for her, is that it?" Persephone asked Aequitas.

"That would suffice. She is not leaving your custody in this place until she finds her pathway — so, if you are eager to be rid of her, your cooperation to assist her will best serve your objective."

Persephone was silent, so I thought Aequitas must've succeeded with his argument.

Athene abruptly raised her head. I could tell she had a plan.

"Laura came here on the songs of Orpheus," she said.

I was happy somebody had finally called me by name.

"And she has come to the temple of the Olympians."

"So?" Persephone said, encouraging her.

"So we must play out the ritual and evoke the ways of old."

Apollo smiled warmly.

"She'll be pleased," he said. "She hasn't been called upon for so long — in a manner that does her this credit again at least."

"Who?" I asked sheepishly.

"The Priestess of Delphi," he answered.

"Oh," I said.

The glow in Apollo's face could've taken the tarnish off silver.

"Is she at this place now?" Aequitas asked.

"No," he said. "But she's only a short distance away, down at the foot of the Royal Pier, in a stall along the seaside promenade. She has a business there."

"A business?" I asked.

"She is a fortune teller."

What else?! I thought.

"We will go there now," Athene said.

No time like the present, I thought, suddenly feeling propelled through a hastily-written script.

There didn't seem to be much dialogue, at least. I mean, they'd brought the Goliath all the way here through the ether, just for this? To carry me to the seaside?

At once it all seemed like a dream, while assuredly taking place in crisp, worldly reality.

They all got to their feet, and we were on our way.

The Muses stayed behind with Festus. I went with Aequitas, Apollo, and Athene down to the seaside.

I had to stay on his back to leave the music hall. He could handle me with ease. I didn't ask what might happen if I tried to get off. I just "couldn't." One of the immutable laws of the universe, like you can't walk through walls, or how Coca-Cola will fizz up your nose if you shake the bottle as you lift it to drink.

We had only four or five blocks to walk. It was just before noon, and the main stem was bustling with shoppers. Must have been a market day.

It was lovely at the seaside — a bright, sunny day, as the first morning light in the junkyard had promised. There was a fresh wind along the promenade, and the tide was high, with waves rhythmically breaking against the sea wall. The pier was huge and impressive, moving out into the ocean in a great broad curve with a walkway twelve or fifteen feet wide, down from which on either side the breakwater dropped away, with what looked like a round dance hall prominent at the far end.

The Priestess's concession was just off the public pathway; a circular tent striped in bold colours, with a frilly edge at the top crest. A sign was propped up on a spindly easel beside its entry: *Fortune Telling, 1/3* in colourful script, with a picture of a crystal ball hand-painted on one side of the lettering.

The great oracle, only one shilling and threepence!

The tent was spacious inside, or seemed so until Aequitas and I passed the threshold and Athene pulled the canvas door closed.

The Priestess was alone when we arrived. Waiting for a client, new or old, to wander in. She didn't look happy. She was pretty though, her dark hair tied up in a bun, wearing a sequined gown in bright colours — as you might expect to find adorning a seer — which flowed unbroken from the collar and sleeves to her ankles.

We all stood facing her, seated at a little round table covered with a tasseled cloth, on which rested the promised crystal ball. It was about five inches in diameter, sitting on a handsome footed brass stand. I could see that it was real crystal, made of flawless hand-polished mineral quartz, not lead glass.

"Priestess," Apollo said reverently.

Suddenly her gloomy face altogether brightened! Half with surprise and half with delight, I think. She reached up and pulled two long pins out of her hair, releasing it to fall onto her shoulders and back.

She knew then why we had come. And, as Apollo predicted, she was visibly pleased.

"We have come to hear your counsel."

"Step forward," she said.

We only had about six inches available to us in the crowded tent, but we made the gesture.

"It concerns the woman there with Aequitas the Mycenaean. Her name is Laura."

Then Apollo was silent. I expected one of them to offer more information, explaining who I was or what I was doing there. But they didn't.

This *was* the latter-day Oracle of Delphi after all.

She spoke.

She knew the truth.

My eyes were fixed to hers.

She spoke to me. Just a few sentences. Mysterious.

"Laura, the mind you now know as your own is the very reality, the all-good — and is, in its true nature, empty. Go to the fearful ambush of your transformation without awe for the sights and sounds you hear. Recognize all worldly phenomena to be reflexions of your own inner life."

She paused and added, "The pain rising in your heart is borne of your continuations gone by."

Then she raised her hand.

My heart grew knotted. I understood and remembered then.

I knew my choices. I knew I had already chosen.

But, the universe is so vast! Worlds upon worlds! How can I know where to go? How can I know where to look? Why should I even try?

"Has he truly loved me?!" I said. "Does he love me now?!"

"Is this knowledge your foremost concern?" she asked.

I wasn't processing very well, but answered as well as I could. I remembered a vague confidence that — like a person out of hypnotic trance — the first words you blurt out are the meaningful article, and clung to that.

"Yes," I said.

Next I learned she was a sorceress in truth. Apollo had seemed a little patronizing, as though merely humouring her.

But he wasn't.

The inside of the tent went unnaturally dark, and her amulet glowed eerily bright.

"Gaze in," she said. "Fall in."

I gazed.

I fell.

As I fell, I saw things. Familiar things. Old things. People and places. I heard my voice arise in my thoughts, but they were not my own thoughts. Instead, it was like another, removed part of myself was presenting them to me.

At first these thoughts, my inner voice, seemed to lack emotion. But I realized this distance was in my hearing, the cool detachment of death.

1979

"It's thirty-four years since he's been gone, Josie."

Josie was a darling friend. We'd been inseparable since Geoff was killed.

It seems strange now to say he was "killed." Like it was either murder or accident, instead of illness or old age. Whereas it was none of those things. War is its own category, and different referents are observed in wartime. Life is different. Death is different.

So many are dying, after all.

"Yes," she answered, raising the teacup to her lips. "It seems like yesterday."

I forgave her the wild cliché.

The morning sun was soothing. I loved this house, especially the front morning room, with its two wide bay windows rising from the floor full to the ceiling, in front of which Josie and I often sat, sharing talk and hot tea to start the day.

The house was decorated and furnished when Geoff and I moved in. It had been built about 1820 — not terribly old for England — then renovated in 1931. It was a short way up a shallow hill on the east side of Exeter, near the university. We came up from London to stay in 1936.

The King was dead, long live the King.

Then in 1945, Geoff was dead.

"So young," Josie said. "He was so young."

He was forty-one in 1945. I was forty-three. Now I'm seventy-seven. Imagine!

It wasn't very long ago that any mention of Geoff would bring a flood of tears to my eyes. I can speak of these things more evenly now, but it is not that my heart has gone cold. Nor has our famous British reserve stiffened my sensibilities — although it does invade the conversation between Josie and me, exaggerated by a certain formality in the language of my own thoughts.

My equanimity has come instead from growing older. With each passing year, I increasingly found peace about a number of things, including the War, and Geoff's death in particular.

As well, lately I've learned I haven't long to live myself. This had a peculiar way of levelling the field between us on his loss.

"Come now, Lilly," she added, "let's talk of happier things."

"Imagine, I've been in this house for forty-three years!" I said.

"The garden has grown up so nicely," she replied.

Everyone did their duty during the War, most with conviction. Geoff joined the civil defense. His job was defusing unexploded bombs. You might think people joined the civil defense to avoid service, but not those with the bomb squad. It was dangerous work, and unpleasant in the extreme. The gelignite — which had to be removed from the shell housings — had a powerful ammonia smell that tore at your nostrils and burned your skin. And, of course, from time to time the bombs would explode. Many men were lost.

Geoff lasted more than three years, from the spring of 1942 until the summer of 1945. With the war in Europe coming to an end then, I thought we might escape — that he might survive, and our lives together would resume.

"Yes, it's lovely. Geoff was a great one for gardening."

She smiled, and I saw the humour. The first words from me after she tries to change the subject are back to Geoff again. It wasn't always like that. He often came to mind, but days or weeks might pass without a word about him between us.

This time she gracefully decided not to resist.

"I can't remember now, Lilly," she said, "did you have a garden at your house in London?"

"No, apart from the window boxes. It was a small property."

"But in Bloomsbury! Surrounded by artists and writers. I'm always envious when you talk about them."

"It was a blessing. Having the friends we did enriched our lives greatly, and all of that happened to us by chance. A number of the people we knew have become quite famous."

I'd said this to her before, probably several times. Our conversation was slipping into a formal tone. At least in that role I could let out some of my pent-up past again if I wanted to, although there was nothing new to say.

"Oh my, yes. You've said before how they loved Geoff."

"Geoff had a gift with people. Not only his friendliness, but he had a way of helping — nay, healing people's lives as well. Something of a mystical talent."

Josie knew this from experience. Geoff had healed her life before the War.

"He never wanted anything in return. He would just say, 'We are in the hands of God,' with that glow in his eye."

"Yes," Josie said.

"Funny, though. Most of the close friends we had among the artists were in Paris, not in London. Our friends in London were more like a discussion circle, or dinner club, rather than close confidants. But still enriching to us."

"Then came the War," she said.

"Everyone's lives were disrupted, of course. And, with Geoff dying, I never renewed those friendships after it ended. Especially those on the continent. Some in London have kept in touch with a card or a letter now and then."

43

"It wasn't that they were Geoff's friends and not your own."

"No, certainly not. Geoff was the first to encourage me to be in-dependent, to be known as a person of substance and express my own views."

This time she forgave me the clichés.

"Even to model for some of the artists!"

"Yes! Which I enjoyed greatly. About that, I'm glad Geoff was so gifted. He knew he didn't have to worry — while I was usually keeping most of my clothes on regardless. Oh my. I loved him completely. I was so happy to have someone to love like that, who was worthy of the devotion, and always repaid it so richly."

I could see Josie's attention had drifted a little when I started talking about love.

"Didn't he fly on a bombing raid once — to Berlin?"

This we hadn't talked about for thirty years.

"It was Hamburg," I answered. "The first big bombing of Hamburg. I was never so worried the whole of the War as I was that night. He didn't have to go. A friend at the Cathedral was in the R.A.F., and had been back home on leave after five missions."

"It was good to survive that many!" Josie blurted out. "Seems horrible to say now. But the casualties for the bomber crews were so very heavy."

"Yes, they were. Geoff's friend — he was called Moore, I can't remember his Christian name — survived another five missions, but then was wounded and lost a foot. He did ground duty after that."

"An unfortunate mercy."

"Yes, quite. The bomber service was like that — odd in a number of ways. Soldiers at the front were away for months or years at a time, whereas the air crews were back in England each morning. Back to nightclubs and women and beer. If they got back."

"So many didn't," Josie added. "Many nights, most of the air-men did not. Or, they were captured after bailing out and spent the duration as prisoners-of-war."

"Geoff flew the Hamburg campaign to see what it was like. He was curious and eager to learn. An unusual experience, like going on that bombing raid, was learning for him."

"Pretty high stakes that time," Josie said.

We grew accustomed to high stakes during the War. Moreover, to a high level of psychic shock, day after day, with little time to collect ourselves, or to mourn. In peacetime, the nation goes into mourning if a gas leak explosion kills a handful of schoolchildren. During the War, people were buffeted with shocks many times that order every day, sometimes of a scale and nature that challenged our base perception of the physical world, such as dropping the atomic bombs over Japan. Or, in Europe, whole cities and their populations incinerated overnight, like Dresden. Even when the War was over, there were unimaginable shocks in store, in particular when the Nazi death camps were liberated.

"I didn't think his flying that raid was worth it. But I knew he would — and could — go only once, provided he came back from the one. Geoff had too much conflict about killing otherwise."

"He didn't think the cause was just?" Josie asked, somewhat incredulous.

"He had no conflict about that! 'There is no slaughter of innocents in the name of God,' he'd say. 'And, of any cause, least of all to further the Aryan race.' This without knowing the fate of the Jews. He just knew that Hitler had to be stopped, with all military force. But he didn't want to be killing people himself, if he could help it. Defusing bombs was without any of that."

We paused then, sharing a smile between us.

It made me happy to recall those moments with Geoff again. A deep, heartfelt, warm, and satisfying happiness, that wanted no other expression.

"Would you like more tea?" Josie offered.

"Yes, thank you. And thanks again for the tea service, Josie!"

"Do you really like it?"

Josie had arrived that morning with a gift for me, a new Royal Winton tea service. A teapot, four cups and saucers, creamer, and sugar, in rose.

Winton wasn't the best fine china by any means, but it was a favourite of mine. The washes they used to tint the surfaces were pleasing to me. This new set was a soft pink with small rosebuds at the handle joins. I had another set in pale yellow, which Geoff had given me.

"Yes, thank you! I like it very much."

"I didn't see any evil landscapes for you today."

After the War and through the 1950s, Royal Winton produced a number of squarish eight-inch free-drawn plates for collectors, having the most peculiar designs improvised by staff painters at the factory. Josie watched for these plates and would buy any she saw that were suitably wretched or bizarre. One day early on I'd referred to one as an "evil landscape," which name stuck for all.

"We laughed so hard seeing the one in Istanbul!"

In 1951 Josie and I had taken a holiday trip to Istanbul, on the famous *Orient Express*.

"That was such a happy time," she continued. "Not neglecting Geoff's passing, you've enjoyed more pastimes and pleasures than most in your life."

"That's true, Josie. And I'm happy we've shared so many."

"You and Geoff lived full lives."

"We did. Something about that used to trouble Geoff. Now and then he'd say something — once, I remember, at a choir rehearsal at the Cathedral. I'd irreverently sat myself on the Dean's bench to listen. The church was otherwise empty, but for Geoff and the choir. At the first rest interval he came over and sat beside me. He said we'd been together so very long, but that this time our lives on an income, flirting with artists and writers, was arising as a setback. Or, at best, a pleasant interlude."

"And you don't know what he was trying to say?" Josie asked.

"I knew Geoff was a sensitive person and let it go."

"I can see how evil landscapes might impair our career in high English culture," Josie said, trying to make a joke. "They certainly had a laugh in Turkey!"

"Ha, ha, yes!" I said. "Trying to be so kind toward us, recommending a Winton artist plate as fine English pottery."

I laughed out loud, and Josie joined me.

Laughter is so refreshing, especially when it is light and has no victim; even if the comedy wouldn't be understood by anyone but those present, sharing the instant. Tears were coming down Josie's cheeks.

"I haven't thought of this in ages."

"The clerk was quite surprised when I actually bought it."

"Shocked, more like it! He took your first offer!"

"I'm still moved remembering the boy outside," I said, suddenly sobering the tone again, though not unpleasantly.

"Yes!" Josie said. "I was appalled. Risking his life for a penny. It made me want to give him half-a-crown. I wish we had, now."

When we came out of the market with the Winton plate we saw a Turkish beggar-boy hanging by one leg down a sewer in the trolley gutter! He'd spotted something below the grate, a penny it turned out. We were moved to pity at how poverty could urge a person to risk so much for so little, especially a small boy, whose family could not provide for him.

He recovered the coin nonetheless, at all peril. Then, seeing us on the sidewalk, he ran over to recommend his services. He didn't know much English, naturally, but he did know some. Enough to negotiate a fee, or to beg for food or money.

"He was so relaxed about the risk he'd taken," Josie said. "What was it he said about it?"

Oddly, the boy evidently was Hindu.

"He said, 'Waiting for you, Englishm'am, passing time until you come out. In between, Lord Krishna took me where I need.' "

1902

Got 'em out. They'll be safe. On the wagons. Oh damn. Lie down. I'll lie down. Good bunk. What a comfy bunk. Just for a minute. Yes, I'll stay inside, just for a minute. Catch my breath. Slow down. Keep talking. That's what they say. Keep talking. Stay awake. Wagons moving out soon. Shut the garrison, he said. That's better. Easy does it. Yes. That's better. Easy. Legs up. That's it. Rest. I'll just rest here a minute. Then call. Call the medic. My hands, wet. Sticky. Blood. You're soaked in your own blood, son. I know that, sir. Water. Bring this soldier some water. Damn this wretched thirst. Kitchener's on the way. There you are, Private. Get this man into the surgery, on the double! Yes sir, Lieutenant! Rest now. Kitchener's coming. He said, British suzerainty in the Transvaal. That's what he said. Damned curious word, that. Suzerainty. Suzie. Oh, Suzie. My delightful Suzie. Took a few slugs. Blast those Boers. They'll fix me up soon. I'll be there soon, Suzie. Just a couple slugs. They'll have 'em out soon, and a medal for me, Suzie, you'll see. Said I'd have one, didn't I? The Sergeant always wore his two medals, one flattened. Saved his knickers he said, the medal took a bullet. My fat gut'll cover me, sir. Ha, ha. Can take a few there in comfort, sir. Oh, Suzie. You'll see, a D.S.C. for that, Suzie. Barely twenty, and a D.S.C. Got those men out, that's the main thing. So tired now. Damn it's quiet. No shooting. Alone now. To Weston-super-Mare, sir. Ma'am. Mrs. Churchill, ma'am. No more action for this service-man, Corporal. Kitchener's ordered this man to the hospital ship. The Churchill ship, sir. Send this man to Weston-super-Mare. Yes, sir. Didn't know you'd do your service in this damn dry scrub desert, did you Private? No sir, Sergeant. Well done, Private. You saved men from real distress. You see, it's your mistress, Suzie. Beatrice, your mistress. Sir Rene passed away while you were fighting in Africa, and my mistress wants to see you, George. Thank you for ask-ing for me, your ladyship. You look beautiful. How beautiful you are. Dear George, call me Beatrice. When I'd see you in the market, Beatrice, I loved you, just looking in your eyes. All my life I loved you, from afar, Beatrice. When you'd say hello to me on the street, and we'd talk briefly, my spirit was standing behind you, threw its arms around you, and held you tight. I loved you too, George, my red-haired boy, and love you still. Now you're home and a hero of the War, George, I hope you'll stay with me. With Suzie and me, George. Please stay. I will, Beatrice. I love you. You look so tired, George. Why don't you sleep. Sleep now. Kitchener will be along soon. He'll move you to the ship. I'll wait for you, George. While you sleep. Sleep now. Sleep.

1883

This year went 214 days without rain in the central region, so dry we could not pass and had to turn back. Had to go by sea.

We had a few moments together, close, as I drifted into the dream between worlds. He could move his mind to those worlds, freely. Many or most of his people could. I was ashamed when I realized it was him at the end, for the thoughts that had passed through my mind, earlier, at our first meeting. He'd come on hire, for my travel inland from Adelaide, into the desert, a guide and porter. Such a long time, walking, walking, so hot, so dry. He cared for me. Wherever I went, whatever I did, secretly watching over me. Always in shadow, ensuring I was safe.

He knew it was me. But for me, instead, he was native, a darkie. An Englishwoman of my class and standing could not be social with a native. Or, would not, with propriety. I was ashamed later but did not know how I might escape that rigour at the time, which also prevented him from saving me from the grisly, iniquitous death I met at the end, finally arrived at Perth by sea. He was not allowed to come inside the public house there. The first amusement I'd had for so many months, a drink at an English club, such as it was. The town was just a rabble of shacks. The first Englishman had only arrived there, on the far west coast, in 1801, eighty-two years before me. I don't think I was intended to drink the fatal cocktail, which instead was meant for one of the loathsome rakes hosting me there.

I fled outside, out of the door, as my head began to swim. Left abruptly, distraught.

The aboriginal was out there, outside in the courtyard, waiting, aware that I'd come to a desperate fate. He picked me up in his arms to carry me to the infirmary a mile away. We came face-to-face in the land of dreams before arriving at that relief, although he was strong, and carried me at a brisk pace.

I could feel myself fading. A gradual, creeping numbness, first in my limbs, crawling into my chest, toward my heart. Numbed, my heart would be silenced. Why did the poison work this way? Why not attack the heart first, at once, without the suspense of that slow paralysis? To give me time to weep? Time to regret each step that had brought me to that remote place? Time to relish the tragic irony of my quest? Time to swim in the polluted thoughts the toxin carried to my brain? It was adequate time for all of these things.

My head swam still, although for some time I was worse, delirious. As we talked in dream, I asked him about things uninvented, cabs self-propelled, without horses, and fast ships. I was to sail again, out of Perth, to home, the next day, and was pointlessly trying to suggest other means, other vehicles for my return. He gently explained, more than once, that I would not make that voyage.

I remembered then our long acquaintance, nay, our long love, and rejoiced to know my quest had been true, but cursed and lamented its bitter outcome. To everything he assured me in loving kindness, with a strong, austere face.

I was only twenty-five years gone a month. As I recovered my bearing, as the life was leaving me, I reflected on how I'd come to that place.

How I'd travelled from England, looking. Not restlessly looking, not discontented, though I did not know what I might be looking for. But I had the sense, the profound sense, there was something to be found. Something necessary to find, to complete myself. I did not know if that might be the love of a man, or woman, or religious awakening, or the awe of nature. I did not have a vision, like Joan of Arc, urging me to go. No angel came to me in my garden, instructing me of a higher cause to pursue. But I felt it in my heart regardless, and bid my heart to guide me.

My father would never have permitted me to sail alone, to make the long passage to Australia on a merchant frigate, even in the company of the ship captain's wife to ensure my safety, to protect my well-being from the threat of hungry seamen, who instead treated me with courtesy and thoughtful regard over the weeks at sea. I carried enough money — taken from my estate trust without my father's knowledge, on the confidence of my solicitor — that I did not worry for any provision once arriving at the colony.

I did not know my final destination either, but took clues from providence. On landing in Adelaide, I met a couple, a man and woman, both young and vigorous and full of courageous ambition, who intended to ranch animals to the north, away from the risk and stigma of the penal colonies. They asked what my own intentions were, and I said to travel the land, so they invited me to go north with them, to Uluru, and then to Stuart, now called Alice Spring, which territory they wished to explore before returning to settle in the more fertile land southeast of Uluru.

We set out with another two men of their acquaintance, and in Port Augusta hired some natives to show us the way and to help with our supplies and baggage animals. Our plan was to follow the new telegraph wire the long way to Stuart. The natives could not under-stand the telegraph line. Why the fleet of tall posts across the land? Was this a fence, a single strand of wire hung high in the air?

I do not remember my expectation for the length of the excursion. Whatever that may have been, the time was far exceeded. We were weeks on foot in the desert. I did not realize the profit to my soul was in getting there. That I would realize the goal of my longing in the travelling, not in the arrival. Like Arjuna, in the *Bhagavad Gita*, the Hindu holy book, when he realizes his chariot driver is Lord Krishna himself, who counsels him that victory in battle was not the article for him that day, rather the waging of war.

Our travel was very difficult. It is a vast desert, past the fertile coastland in the east, with little relief of either heat or thirst, and little punctuated by any settlement. The coach does not stop at the public house in the next village, with yard-glasses of ale and warm rooms with clean linens at hand, and servants to fetch water in the night. It is a deep, unrepentant wilderness.

I'd gone, ladylike, in a full day dress, but within two days' walk had shed that fabric in favour of my petticoat alone. Themselves going mostly naked, the natives little understood my dress-wearing in the first place, but found the appearance of my undergarments utterly comical. Not for any indecency, which was alien to them, but instead for their unnatural proportions, the tight waist and long laced top, in contrast to its billowy leggings.

We brought ample supplies of rice, but only occasionally came on sufficient free water to boil it with, instead having moisture from roots the natives would dig up from below the ground, or stiff tubers stuck down into it, that would draw a few drops for each of us. We ate other scrub plants and sometimes rodents or insects they would find to cook. I was prepared in mind and determined to survive on the land by the local custom.

After some weeks' time, however, we had to turn back. There had been no rain whatsoever and sources of moisture became too scarce for our survival. The return journey seemed twice as long, and twice the ordeal, of our way out. I still did not know what it was that I sought, but the urge to persevere remained in my heart.

Returning to Adelaide, my travelling companions, whose yearn-ing for adventure was not at all discouraged — indeed, remained keen — suggested we go by ship to Western Australia, to Perth. Something in the sound of the word resonated in my heart. That is where I was to go. Perth, like an anthem. I'd heard the word in a dream. So I agreed, and we went together. I had abundant funds and could meet my share of the hire easily. To my great surprise, two of the natives volunteered to come along, although their people were unaccustomed to travel by sea. Most in their acquaintance had never seen a sea-going ship, much less made a long voyage. But they came regardless. My protector came. He recommended that he should, that his guidance and knowledge would be useful in the west-land, despite the unpleasant prospect of ocean travel.

1858

"Mr. Lindsay, blindfold me please," I said.

He laughed sweetly — his low-voiced laugh, from his heart — and answered, "I don't think we're well enough for that, dearest."

"I know," I said. "But I want to lie with you in the same way, as we would years ago. I want to talk."

"We can sit by the fire and talk, angel," he said, with a hint of a tear at the corner of one eye. "We've always been able to talk."

"Yes, we have, love. Always. But I'd like to lie with you there, like we used to. When we'd be close."

"All right, then," he said. "I'd like that too."

We went into the bedroom. He helped untie my fittings, and I pulled down my dress, folding it over the chair. I lay on the bed in my underslip.

Without a word he tied my eyes around, as I'd asked, and lay beside me, holding me gently in his strong arms.

"Do you remember the poem you wrote for me?" I asked.

"Certainly, my love. It's the only poem I ever wrote, a poor effort indeed."

"It was not a poor effort for me, Mr. Lindsay."

"A comedy is what I intended," he said with a soft laugh. "You often asked me my thoughts, or to assure you on this thing or that. Clarence at the market helped me with some of the words."

"I knew that, Mr. Lindsay, but it was not a syllable less your own. Can you say your poem now?"

He said his poem.

Our lives all were oars and nets,
And strong winds, that billowed the long
Linen skirt you'd hand-stitched at evenings.
Your old skirt plain stitched,
Your plain face my strength,
Your words plain like iron nails.
After we ate, you'd say, "Good Mr. Lindsay,
Speak man, and tell me your gravest thought."
And I'd answer, "This be that, Mrs. Lindsay,
No fish were ever better cooked than these."

"We probably haven't long now, Mr. Lindsay," I said.

"I know that's true, angel. Though Doctor Kermode said it's not an unhappy finish, passing from this consumption. He said a great repose comes over a person at the end."

"I'm glad we're ill with this together. I would like my life to go on, but only with you."

"Aye, that is my own happiness as well. We've had a good life."

"Many don't get past forty years," I said. "We're three years more along and cannot complain."

"I would tell you plainly, I've been happier for each year with you than twenty times each without."

"I know that's true," I said. "I know you speak the truth — and that would be the full truth of my heart as well."

He held me close and kissed me on the neck. I loved to feel him touch me there.

Years before, when we were young, I'd whisper to him when he held me close, in Manx. *Va ny creeaghyn ain cha kenjal lesh yn gerjagh va ain cooidjagh. Nagh geayll shin rieau lheld roie, as scoan my nee shiu arragh.* Which would be in English, *Our hearts are so mellow with our pleasure together. You never heard such before, and you scarce will again.*

We were only simple country people, but we loved one another. Some may think the love of simple people is in some way lesser than that of nobles or merchants, but it is not. It's as full as any felt by any other man and woman on earth, as rich as the sweetest words Mr. Dryden could in his life conceive.

"You've worked hard, and God knows it's so, Mr. Lindsay," I said. "Every day out with your brother in the boat; then, after pulling in heavy nets for hours on end, hauling the catch to market."

"I've had Len to help me, and young Marcus at market."

"He's done you both well and honest, Marcus has," I said.

"After Robbie pulled such a bad turn those years back."

"Don't be thinking of that, Mr. Lindsay. It's long gone by and will only make your heart sore to consider it again."

"I won't, and I don't dwell on it. I haven't for a long while now anyway."

"It's been a good living, and I'm grateful to you."

"I'm as grateful to you, for the house and home you've kept. Always a warm fire burning, good food to eat, well-tailored clothes to wear, and healthy pigs and sheep in the yard. If the truth were known, it'd be you they'd say had the greater labour."

"Nay, the truth'd be we've had hours together upon each day to our leisure, enjoyed with friends at evening at the Old Mine House, or sat by our fireside."

"Or out under the night sky," he added.

"Yes," I said, smiling warmly. "That was a great pleasure to me, Mr. Lindsay."

"And to me. I enjoyed your learning, angel. Knowing what was what among the stars above and telling me so much while we'd lie on the hillside. I valued that."

"Thank you for saying so, Mr. Lindsay."

"I would say so at the time, love."

"Yes, you did — while you did not believe me about the giant."

"Worse than that, I do not recall any story of giants now!"

"I don't recall hearing of more than one giant, but the one was a giant in truth. We saw the marks of his hands impressed on the tops of great standing stones."

"I remember, of course. I was confused at what you meant a moment ago."

"Yes, I meant that in the field at Balla Keeil Pherick, on the way from Sloc to Colby. There were five stones in the ancient days, each marked in the same way by the giant as he threw them down from the top of Cronk yn Irree Laa."

"Where we went to see the stars the once."

"Aye."

"There's none other on the Isle of Man who knows as much about the night sky as you, my love."

We lay silent for a few minutes.

"We've seen so little of the world, Mr. Lindsay."

"Nonsense, love," he said with a smile, "we've been up around the north coast together each year, and across through the hills many times."

"The Isle of Man is not the world," I said, trying not to sound dour. "There are so many other lands, far across the seas."

"None in our acquaintance has been across the seas. Nay, even in England and Wales only men joining the merchant marine or Navy service will see faraway lands, and so many return unhappy."

"Tom Cooper returned well in mind."

"Yes, that's true. There'll be some, even the odd one here from Man."

"Those raised in town, more like. From English families."

"Cooper speaks Manx."

"Yes, but still of an English family," I said.

"Yes, true enough."

"Have you given the cabinet to Mrs. Kelly?"

"Yes, I did that. Yesterday, when they both came to help with the garden."

"They've been so kind."

"She was delicate to show they knew my brother would be here at the time, looking after the arrangements. I assured her in turn he was full-knowing of the modest gifts we'd made and had pledged to honour them."

"And he will, won't he?" I asked.

"He surely will, out of love and respect, and somewhat for lack of any desire of his own."

"Len hasn't much temptation for wealth or possessions, it's true!" I said with a laugh. "Bless his heart."

"Nor have we — nor have we much to tempt anyone. But we've been happy in our lives."

"We've had more than we've ever needed."

My lip was trembling.

"Is there something the matter? Something apart from our decline?"

"There is, I think. There's something I have to confess."

His face remained calm. He knew I'd done no great evil.

"What ever could that be?" he asked.

"We've had few amusements, Mr. Lindsay."

"What amusements have we possibly missed?"

"I mean merriment. Fun. We haven't had much fun."

"They'd usually call 'fun' some kind of low merriment, love. I wouldn't take your meaning that way."

"No, I don't mean low pleasure."

"Nor can it be the humour we'd have between us."

"Such as when you'd address me as *mooar-stroinagh*?" he added, and laughed. These were the Manx words for 'large-nosed,' a pet name I'd had for him when we were younger. He'd had that and did still. In truth, as I tell you this entire story in truth, its shape gave his face warmth and dignity.

I paused for a moment, giving him a warm squeeze.

"Do you remember when we were at Douglas eight years ago, and you saw the steam-engined boat in the harbour?"

"Surely, yes. I was fascinated to see it."

"You hadn't seen anything of the like before."

"Nay, never. Brought me delight to see."

"That's what I'm saying by fun. So rarely have we had fun."

"I haven't felt wanting."

"No, naturally not. You're a good man, a hard-working man, and content. But I wished to bring you the pleasure of some amusement. Some fun for us after all our hard work."

"And what brings this to a confession?" he asked smiling.

"My good intentions have had me deceive you."

"How ever be?!" he said with great wonder.

"Take the hem of my dress in your hand," I said, and he reached for it on the chair.

"Can you feel what's sewn in on the side?"

"Two guineas," he answered.

"Yes, that's it. Each year when we've slaughtered the sheep I've skimmed the lanolin and sold it without your knowledge."

"But I have known and not troubled you about it."

"You've known, and not asked after the money?"

"I've known it was in the hem of your dress, as a shilling has gone to two and half-a-crown to a guinea. I've been very happy indeed you've had something for yourself alone there and would never think to question your intention for it."

I couldn't repress my tears at his kindness and gentle spirit.

"I was saving so we could have some fun when we were a little older. That we would have a few shillings to travel somewhere and buy frivolous things."

My tears increased, bringing damp to the blindfold.

"But we won't be able to now. Our time is so short, and we're so unwell. Those two guineas will be buried with me and will've brought us no pleasure or good."

"We're not dead yet."

I was crying such that I had to take my blindfold off. He dried my eyes with it, saying we should go and sit in the other room beside the fire.

Our little house had only two rooms. The bedroom, where we lay, with a large wood-poster bed, one chair, and a dresser. And our living room, with the fireplace at its centre, a kitchen in one corner opposite a tall window beside the door. I'd cut the opening for that window years before, building it up from floor to ceiling in foot-square panes.

We went and sat by the fire.

"Understand me this," he said once we were comfortable. "I would've the same confession to make as you — worse, as I saved more than nine pounds sterling over these years, unknown to you."

"I've always respected your care for our money, Mr. Lindsay."

"By which care I've always given my true earnings to you, for our household expense."

"Still, I wouldn't be surprised or disappointed you'd held some to reserve, sir," I said.

"I'm glad of that, and love you for it."

"So we neither have brought much fun to ourselves on account of our respective conservations."

"Nay, my love, on the contrary, I've spent mine yesterday on an amusement for you, which will arrive at the house tomorrow."

"Goodness, me! What could that be, Mr. Lindsay, you'd think would bring us delight in our infirm condition?"

My voice was sincere and not skeptical.

"It is a telescope, the Gregorian type, of four-and-a-half inches breadth to the mirror. A suitable size for our time together past evening in the garden. I'm assured it's an instrument of good scientific figure, certified at Greenwich, and handsome to see as well, made of brass and wood on a fine mount. Of a value better than my savings, to be sure, except as Len persuaded a seaman who had it in stores how it was for the joy of a dying man near his last days. We might need two guineas to build a shelter for us and the instrument out in back here, that we might spend the deep of late evenings without worry of sudden weather, with good seats to rest our bottoms, and perhaps even a fire."

"Oh, Mr. Lindsay, I am so deeply touched by your kindness. I am so very gratified."

I got up from my chair and sat at his feet, laying my head in his lap, and holding him tightly around the waist with my arm.

"But sir, I would still've wished to take you travelling elsewhere in the world! How dearly I wished to give you this. To have had some fun seeing other places together, where we've never been."

"This be the truth, Mrs. Lindsay, we'll do better than that. We'll soon visit the vast places above — all the stars and moons and planets. As real and great and near to our eye and mind as any hard earth anywhere we might've trod beneath our feet."

1810

I only learned much later what had happened. What happened to him after we were parted.

We both had been so young to begin with, over the short months we had together, but for several years I still relied on my impressions gained at the time. Quirky, unreliable, youthful impressions. Mistaken impressions in part, although there were neither truths nor fictions that could have eased my pain. It hardly mattered what I thought or believed — at bottom, he did not come back and I was left alone with child.

Together, his mother and mine engineered a falsehood with the parish priest here at Lyme Regis. A marriage record was created between him and me, marked for the day before his sailing, in order that I might have his navy pension should he be declared dead, and I thus widowed. In this way, I could live a decent peaceful life thereafter, whatever the outcome. A woman with a child born out of wedlock is forever an outcast. The loyal wife of a navy officer, particularly if separated forever from her loving husband by disaster at sea, is treated with sympathetic regard and has a place in middle society, even if she may not find acceptance to wed again.

I sometimes resented that I spent my passion so vigorously at such a young age, without future opportunity after he was gone, because my passion did not leave me with his disappearance. I can confess now to some incidental secret indulgence at infrequent intervals, but I know he would not disapprove of me for that.

There was no message from him in life. I heard a diary was found attending his remains, but I was not given possession of it, and was past five full years before having formal notice of his death.

We loved only once, which may have been in mystical anticipation of his death by shipwreck, an urgency to have that complete and final bonding at that last and only opportunity. He did not force me in any way, being a decent man, with whom I was wholly assured of our mutual true love since we'd first met. Even so, it was clandestine in another way, as he secreted me aboard his ship, with the ironic knowledge that this was the place of our greatest privacy, the crew ashore drinking or sleeping — but in either case determined to remain on land as long as they were able, with their long voyage to commence the following day — and only two hands' watch on the deck, who played cards and talked over hot cider.

Down in his bunk, nestled in his hammock, we kissed and held each other in silence, and in silence I pulled away my dressing and unbuttoned his own. Feeling his warmth and strength within me brought no shock, instead fulfillment of the most pleasant kind. My heart and soul felt whole in him, which sense remained with me ever after, the whole time I lived.

I gave no thought to the possibility of a child at the time, but it gave me no distress when I knew. On my first firm suspicion, my mother was of greater concern, although her appeal to me was considerate and without reprimand. She knew our hearts were well committed to the other, and he could not be faulted for being so long at sea. For our invented marriage record he would be fully understanding and applaud the measure, knowing my welfare in his absence depended upon it. We did not know then, nor for a long time after, that he was lost at sea, shipwrecked on a foreign coast, and would not return at all.

He never knew he had a daughter, whom I loved well enough for us both, and to whom I always spoke well of her father. I became gravely, nay, mortally ill in my forty-first year, when she was only gone fifteen. Old enough that good and decent principles had been instilled in her, together with a confidence and knowledge of the world sufficient to ensure her future. She was already being courted by a merchant, a man of good means and good character, giving me some peace for her career knowing I'd soon leave her. My mother survived me as well, being at the age of fifty-eight when I fell ill, pledging to care for my daughter when I was gone. I survived several weeks against my fever, but with the outcome yet inevitable.

My mother often marvelled, although without disapproval, at my tenacious waiting, before we had the official notice of his death. Every day I went by the long pier, whether morning or afternoon, and stood for a long time, gazing out to sea in search of his sails. Two or three times in a week I'd see a three-masted cargo frigate and would run to the harbour master, calling, "What is the name of that ship?!" To which he would kindly answer, "The Clarence!" or "a Belgian warship!" but never "Apollo!"

More than once at evening he'd pass me and say, "The Apollo is feared lost, child, off the coast of Burma."

He was trying to tell me, ever so gently, but I could not hear.

It was something more than love. Indeed, the memory of his company so quickly faded. After but a few years I could scarcely summon his face to mind any longer. But his spirit in me was strong, curiously strong, and curiously enduring. Be assured I am of sound mind in saying so, but I felt him embrace me at night. His spirit would seem to shelter me and give me rest.

A retired officer of senior rank, who was a landowner in Dorset, with a house and other properties in Lyme Regis, gave me the use of a cottage at no fee, on promise of occupancy until such time as my daughter was married; even if I should survive him, or she me.

The former turned out to be, a promise which his executor honoured, giving me dignity by renewing the understanding. In turn,
I promised I would add value to the property by good care and
improvements out of my pension, which pledge I kept. It was small,
of three rooms only, but entirely comfortable and well-suited to
the needs of myself and my daughter. After my father died, six years
before my own illness, my mother came to live with us there,
and we were happy and always well-tempered together. We had
a small garden behind, where we grew phlox, daisy, foxglove,
sweet-pea, and other flowers.

The Commodore came to visit monthly. When I became ill, he
sent his ward to see me each day, a Scottish boy of fifteen years,
who was an apprentice distiller for flavoured liquors. Early each
morning he spent an hour to tidy the house and garden, and would
bring me fresh cakes. He made tea when he arrived and served me a
platter in bed on fine white china, a gift from the Commodore.

The boy was charming and cheered me greatly, having generous
and intelligent conversation. Without intending, he brought to
mind how I'd never enjoyed the company of a man in my maturity;
which, when I once said this same thing to him, he replied his
heart wept for my loneliness and expressed his deep regret to cause
me such unhappy thoughts.

I assured him how, on the contrary, a person always mindful of
others first, always generous in their thoughts, as he was, would
so rarely have any regret to carry, neither on the day at hand nor
over the whole of their lifetime. A benefit so little understood!
Moreover, how his visits brought me joy and that my loneliness
contained more poignance than sorrow. He said he was sorry in
any event for being in neglect of my need of company for so long,
before his visits began. We suddenly embraced then on my sickbed;
an innocent embrace, but warm and comforting to me.

My remorse was renewed from time to time after that, for the loss
of my husband, my lover, who never knew we'd been posthumously
wed. When we lay in the hammock that night on board ship, after
we'd loved and his child first began to bud within me, he talked
only of my care — that he'd signed on an ocean vessel, rather than

a channel ship, in order to offer me the prospect of some income. He saw his fortune over distant seas, in teak or gold or spices or tea, and would return to me with his riches, still young and vigorous, then build us a house, where he'd stay with me forever. His voice was even, his ambition true. Indeed, his pledge was only foiled by the cruellest fate, about which he suffered much. I was bound to his fate as my own; but, while his suffering was great, it was mercifully short. My own, while of a milder quality, was long enduring.

I drift back by this time now in dream, as though a landscape in still-life, where in dream I heard a poem from him, left to me as he passed through dying dreams himself years before. A poem in short phrases, as though at his last breath, the moment of each thought condensed in short, faint puffs of air drawn into failing lungs.

You did not know
that you were not
abandoned then,
as you stood by the sea,
watching, waiting
each day for
great white sails
to heave into sight
with your lover,
your heart,
sitting smiling
wide-eyed on
a mizen yard.
You never knew
my ship was wrecked
near the monsoon
coast of Burma,
the hold full of warm
brown teakwood,
all hands lost
save myself, the gunner,

and the captain's wife,
drifting to a hostile
shore, held prisoner
on the narrow beach
by tigers inland,
where I starved
to death.
You did not know
I called for you,
dreamed of you,
wrote letters unsent
to you, begged
your forgiveness for
every small crime
against you, pleaded
if there was
a merciful God
you might hear
me say
goodbye.

1769

Entering my seventy-fourth year, I enter my final year.

I have lived the life I desired to have.

In this life I have made fabrics, coloured with indigo, the finest in all Japan.

Having this original opportunity, then devotedly perfecting it, gave me freedoms which a woman could rarely enjoy in this era.

I have been master of my estate.

Warlords, soldiers, merchants, and clerics have come to visit me, offering me their protection and respect, and all have sat in my room for my ceremonial tea.

I have practiced Shinto but have known the Changes.

I have had the peaceful company of women, and the diligent industry of a silent, devoted husband, who lay with me in the gentle company of my companions.

All my years have passed in the quiet contemplation given by my craft, once given the opportunity.

Before my opportunity, I was dressed and painted each day for male suitors.

My lover opened the means for me to progress.

We were secret lovers. Her mother was a fabric-maker. In me her mother saw the heir to her knowledge, and took me in.

I saw no more suitors then, and my family was honoured by the appointment. I could spend my nights in dignity, resting my face in the soft breasts of my companion and lover.

I could marry a man of genuine close friendship, who understood and approved of the true urges of my heart, but whose family hadn't the social standing to permit his prior courtship.

I had to prove my worth in apprenticeship and worked long years in steady effort.

Long trips down the valley to search and gather the leaves for the dye, then to carefully separate, dry, and precisely mix.

Heavy loads of boiled cloth to carry to the stream to rinse.

Huge bronze vessels to scour.

Intricate folds to tie and knot, often in many repetitions, to create the patterns in the fabric by excluded spaces.

As I worked at these labours I grew in knowledge, unaware of my own learning.

When my master entered the final year of her life, she announced my inheritance to her practice.

I spoke to her privately, respectfully declining my entitlement.

She answered, saying all her knowledge had been given me as I worked, and by my modest disposition I gained command of every subtlety of her craft, method, and talent.

I said I would accept her title and position only if wholly earned, by creating new patterns of original beauty, worthy of her name and estate.

I had not created any original design of any worth and was filled with apprehension even as I heard my own words.

The days passed largely in silence between my loving husband and me throughout our life together, but that evening we spoke.

The night was warm and clear, and we gazed at the stars above us from the porch as we lay together.

"How do I do new work?" I asked him.

"How long have we been together?" he replied.

"Throughout this life," I answered. "And in other times and places, which we have remembered in our dreams."

"How can we live new lives?" he asked.

"The same as we can create new designs," I said comprehending, my heart suddenly aflow with ideas.

1695

It is an ignominious fate to die of drink, even while I've done so at gradual leisure.

A slow decline, born of tragedy.

That this sorrowful event was telling and decisive needs no further elaboration, but I have often resented my idle powerlessness against it.

My home is at Lynmouth, on the south coast of the Bay of Bristol, near enough the mouth of the Severn to sail across the water to the city of Bristol within a day. I live here in a house on the main road above the sea wall, in failing health, with my son and his wife.

My son is a good man, past twenty years. He married Jane, Henry Jackson's daughter from Brighton on the coast in the southeast, eleven months ago. Apart from having his inconsolable mother in the house, the two have been happy and well, though without a child as yet.

Lynmouth is at the foot of the steep cliffside, by which Britain rises up out of the sea. Almost the entire coast of the island is wrapped with this cliff-face, a long wall down to the ocean waves, continuous for mile upon mile, at different intervals sometimes higher and sometimes lower. The rise is particularly great along the Bay of Bristol, where our village is spotted up the hill from the sea wall at the limit of the tide.

Both my husband and I were raised in the village, both of hard-working fathers who drew a meagre living from the sea and hard-working mothers making the best possible advantage of what they had, always grateful we'd escaped the great plague that had lately raged in the cities and towns of Britain, indeed, in parishes not far from us here.

As children we used to explore up above the cliff, roaming far and wide through the fields and sheep lands. Norman and I became steady companions as the years and our childhoods passed, and we had a strong fondness for one another.

All the families of the village were known to each other, as you might expect, and most were on good terms. There were disputes, but it was the custom in our village to strive to resolve them early, before friendships could be poisoned. Norman's father, respected for his learning and wisdom, was a frequent arbiter. If others in the village had a disagreement, outside of felonies of law, they would bring themselves to Norman's father and state their respective cases. He was skilled at negotiating a resolution to each person's satisfaction, and also at making a reasonable explanation of what was right and just for the circumstance at hand and what was not.

When Norman and I had gone ten or eleven years, he began coming with us on Sundays when we went exploring the countryside, outings which brought Norman and me to a closer friendship. With my father's approval and (most uncommonly) that of the Vicar for our absence from church, my mother would pack a lunch basket for the three of us, and I'd put on my walking shoes — having the choice of three pairs of shoes, with another for dress, and a light laced sandal to wear in the boats — then we'd set out before sunrise on the steep walk up the criss-cross road to the top of the cliff.

We'd walk the whole morning then, through grazing fields and across ancient walls and hedges, in the direction of Exmoor. There was a forest glen about four miles distant, where we knew the faeries lived.

We'd stop for lunch there in the glen, usually having some cold cooked venison and cheese and bread, leaving our small sandwich ends for the fair folk, after which meal Norman's father would take us looking for them. Sometimes they showed themselves, flittering through the bluebells and among the vines wrapping the trees, other times not; but, whichever occurred, Norman's father made the quest enchanting by his seriousness and reverence, always speaking to us in a voice and manner as though we were grown.

My mother believed in the faeries also, but always said she hadn't seen any herself since she was a girl. When I came home and told her we'd seen them in the glen — which I'd say only if we had — she believed me and would answer saying she wished she was as young as I again.

From an early age Norman did not wish to be a fisherman, although not from arrogance or sloth. He was wary of the sea for no rational reason, except perhaps as that sentiment was a prophetic one. He persuaded his father to speak to Frank Howson, the village blacksmith, when it became known that an apprentice position was open at his shop. Howson gladly accepted Norman, who was tall with strong arms, and reliable with a personable disposition; an asset worth acquiring.

I confess as well that, after coming to seventeen or eighteen years, I also considered Norman an asset worth acquiring.

He was made a journeyman blacksmith at eighteen, after four years' apprenticeship at Howson's shop, and, getting along well with Howson, and there being enough work, he stayed on there, earning a good wage. They made strong barrel rings for the coopers, fittings for small boats, hardware for doors and windows, handles and hinges for cabinets, and, of course, horseshoes.

From the start, I cautioned Norman about the dangers of the work, and, while I could do nothing about the heat and heavy weights to carry, I persuaded him to roll raw cotton in each ear against the noise. There is such a ferocious noise in a blacksmith's, when they clang their hammers against the iron being worked.

He resisted me at first on this but soon did so regardless, which became a habit, for which later he often thanked me. In the interim, most of the villagers thought he was already mostly deaf. With the cotton in each ear he could hear a conversation only poorly.

Over his apprenticeship, I was acquiring the talents I would need as a wife and home keeper, which entailed a good deal more and varied tasks than any blacksmith, miner, or fisherman. Sewing, spinning, knitting, and darning, to make and repair clothing. All manners of cookery suited to an English palate, including the husbandry of sheep, hogs, and chickens, and also the butchery of those animals, in the likely event the home to which I went had a small stock. As well, the making of soaps and cleansers. And keeping the household accounts, at which my mother excelled and could offer me both technique and insight.

Come the time I wanted to bring Norman home, I felt as worthy of him as he of me. As well, it was meaningful that we were of long and close acquaintance, that his reputation in the village was of the highest integrity, and, not least of all, that he often volunteered the opinion I was attractive to him.

He had to be brought home, regardless, as he gave little thought to women or marrying on his own. Without a nudge from me, we'd have gone seventy years before he took notice he hadn't married.

So, one Saturday evening we had a walk along the seaside. I took his hand and began talking about how I looked forward to having a house of my own, with a good husband to be with me. Somewhat shocked, he asked who it was I intended to marry! I replied, only him, of course, and his face brightened with relief there was none other I loved better.

Perhaps moved by his envy at the possibility, he answered me saying that we ought to be married, him and me. I could see it flash through his brain that he'd better observe the usual custom, and was immediately down on one knee to ask my hand in marriage in a more formal manner. He twisted a piece of wire he found in his pocket to make a ring for me, and when I consented he placed the same on my hand, with a promise to replace it with better as soon as it could be made.

This promise he made good, creating a handsome gold wedding ring with his own hands at the smith, though I kept the iron wire and have it still, every once in a while giving it a little wax and a rub to keep it from rusting.

Norman's uncle offered us the house left vacant and well-furnished by his cousin's death two years before, there being no other heir to the property. We agreed on a price which was both modest and fair — I think still a generosity on his uncle's part. Howson gave Norman some money toward our initial payment as a bonus for finishing his apprenticeship so productively for the shop. Norman produced the rest we needed from his own savings, which included a legacy of more than three pounds sterling he'd had from his aunt as a child. Norman's parents gave us a handsome sum as a wedding present, which we used to make repairs and improvements, including a new roof, and to acquire some livestock. My parents, not as well situated as Norman's, were equally generous to their means, giving us a pony and cart.

Norman enjoyed his married life. He had little knowledge of what would be expected of him; but, while naïve in this regard, he responded with interest to every suggestion and made a consistent effort to improve our welfare. Our lives together were quickly settled into a happy method of things.

We rose at the six o'clock bell — struck by the sexton at the parish church, who had a good mechanical clock in his rooms to remind him of the hour — and went about our household chores. Norman would feed the pony and livestock, most years being a pair of hogs and some chickens, and cleaning their stalls and pens. While he attended these tasks, I cleaned the hearth and started the kitchen fire to make our morning meal, for which I'd work fresh dough and set it to bake, put red pork to spit, and walk down to the public house for a quart of ale. While I was bringing our meal to table, Norman would make a repair to the house or do some other needed task. Then, after eating, and within an hour and a half of our rising, he'd be off down the road to the smith, and I would start my laundering, cleaning, and clothes-making, as our need dictated. Evenings we had an hour, or usually two, at our leisure, to join our friends at the public house, or have guests to our kitchen to play cards, or sometimes have a walk by the sea.

I had learned to read as a girl and would often pass the evening with a book, if I had the loan of one from a neighbour. Or from the Bible, which alone we owned ourselves. Norman would often ask me to speak the words aloud, so he could have pleasure in the story also. He was less keen on hearing poems, unless it was Mr. Donne, whose romantic air he liked. Norman was tender in private, but little given to speaking this way between us of his own.

Four years and six months went by before I became with child, which time I was happy to have, and which child was then an un-conditional joy in our lives. I was well-prepared to care for our boy, whose childhood passed with caring attention and the protec-tion of his interests. He was well-behaved and brought us much delight. Before long he was helping with our chores, which came not so much as a relief of those labours but as a bonding of spirits in the events of our lives.

All of our friends and family would remark how intelligent and well-mannered the boy was. He had a healthy body as well, and took naturally to the boats. When he was five years old, Norman made him a rowboat of his own.

Every afternoon, weather and waves allowing, my son was out in his rowboat, pulling at the oars mile after mile. He gained a good sense of the sea as he rowed, and after a few years' time also gained great strength and bulk. His family and friends would say that Norman was the only man in the village with chest and arms more massive than my son's.

As he grew older, his interest grew stronger, and his knowledge also. He learned the principles of navigation and practiced the skill. As he learned to read, he borrowed books of the narratives of great sea voyages, from which he gained both the excitement of adventure and the genuine education of the details of their undertaking.

The smith was prosperous, and when my son was fourteen years old, Norman was able to provide materials for a new, larger boat, with a mast and keel for sails. My son built the boat himself, which patient and diligent labour occupied him for thirteen months before it was complete. Once launched, the new boat was handsome and strong and pulled well in the wind.

We had no prospect of any other trade for him and thought he might be called to a naval institute for officer training. But later on he declined that opportunity in favour of providing refuge for me. I was grateful, but had made no encouragement of the boy to forego an education. My sister would have taken me in. Even so, he decided to pursue a course of lesser wealth, building boats.

His effort amounted to founding a new shop, in which endeavour two of his friends joined him. They were considerate partners to each other and were soon building small boats of both integrity and value, gradually coming to good reputation in all the towns along the coast. The success of their business was also a benefit to Norman, as he took a new apprentice and also built a new bellows to meet their needs for iron parts and fittings.

My courage fails me now, as I write. I was next going to describe the outings we had in my son's boat. I have told our history to this point with an even mind, but now the outcome of my story becomes the outcome of my life, and I can scarcely proceed.

I suppose I can wring out the essentials of it, as I've managed to wring out my days since, but I can already see my happy narrative falling into ruin, even as my life fell into ruin then.

I'd sailed with my son to Bristol, where he was showing the boat for sale, and where I could buy some fabric and other goods that couldn't be had in Lynmouth. As we returned, about halfway back as evening was coming upon us, a tremendous storm came up, a fifty-year storm, and the wind and waves at sea were great. When Lynmouth lights came into sight, my son could no longer tack aside the gale and turned us into the wind. We both lay in the bottom of the boat, often washed over with cold, heavy waves.

Norman could see us from shore in the dim light and took my son's rowboat into the water. With the extraordinary power in his arms and chest he made distance toward us, which no other man in the village had the might to do, a strength enhanced by his love for us, which fired his heart and steeled his resolve to pull his oars to breaking against the tempest.

SOME SUNNY DAY : 1658

We tipped suddenly as he came upon us, and I was cast into the cold water with much alarm. Norman jumped from his boat and I soon felt his arms around me, holding me so I could breathe and swimming vigorously to the sailboat, which my son had righted and was bailing, though he was tangled in a line. My body was shocked with the cold sea. I coughed and gagged with swallows of water, and my mind was distraught.

This memory has persistently haunted my dreams ever since and causes me fresh anguish with every recollection.

Norman heaved me into the boat and pulled himself up behind me. He made a broken spar fast beneath a cross-member for me to hold, to which I clung for life.

Then he moved to help my son from the sheet halyard in which he'd become tangled, when the truck suddenly came away, striking Norman hard on the knees, both weights then swept sliding over the gunwale into the sea.

My son was helpless to come to his aid, and Norman's strength was finished.

In surviving this ordeal, I was not a person rescued. I was not saved to my joy, or to any benefit, but rather to my loss and long despair.

I put my hand out to him, but I could not reach. As he was pulled away by the sea, I heard him call *"Slane ayd, ainle,"* which means *Goodbye, angel* in the Manx Gaelic.

1658

Men do not grow close in spirit to their women on our island. How different it is from truth, living in high caste in this pleasant place of natural abundance, but to have our hearts remain distant.

He kidnapped me and brought me to the men's house when I was newly at womanhood. This was the custom for those native to Yap, and it was an honour to be taken, especially by a brave warrior of his standing. He was loyal to me the whole time of our lives, and remained strong, never dropping caste by lost conflict and steadily gaining wealth through courageous deeds. He gave protection to his tenants and was respected in other villages. We had large canoes, and I had the finest baskets in the community.

My husband kept his good standing with the help of six men who lived in his lodge. They never took wives, but were happy, and they had the company of women when they needed. When my husband was challenged to warfare, they put on soldiers' dress and went to fight with him. When there was no challenge, they gathered copra and betelnuts, fished the ocean, and built houses and walkways.

My husband ate with the men, eating food below his caste. He and his men ate eel, whereas others of his class ate turtle. From a young age my husband said sea turtles were noble creatures and should be left alone and not hunted. None in his family ate turtle. We had giant turtle shells standing inside around the wall of my husband's men's house, but they had not been hunted. My husband gathered these when he was young, finding them empty on the beach. He brought them back to his house with the help of the men, who had recently come into his service. At the house my husband would show them to visitors, saying the lifeless thing was only vain ornament, that the turtle lived long and should live in dignity.

The men came out to paddle the great canoe with my husband when he would go to Palau to quarry stone. They carried back *rai*, as the stone disks were called, of great weight and size. The men knew the sea and its ways, and they knew when to travel and when to wait. They were strong and diligent at their paddles.

I always walked behind them, which is the custom of my people. When we walked together the men set a pace where I could keep up without strain. They walked around my baskets when they were in the yard and would bring me hibiscus flowers for my hair when they saw an attractive blossom along the pathways.

My husband offered them wealth and property for themselves but they always said no. My husband would say they could have *rai* for themselves, to lean against their own houses for their own wealth, but they always said no.

The men stayed with us fifty years, until my husband was old and I was old and our lives were nearly finished. We passed those fifty years with the passage of the new moon only one month ago.

On the night of that new moon, ghosts came to the community house where my husband was sitting alone. They told him to carry the turtle shells from his house down to the ocean. Although he was old and his teeth gone and his jaw bad from the betel and lime, he did as they asked and carried them one by one to the beach, which was not far, but it still took him all night to do.

He put each shell in a tidepool, finding there were six large tidepools formed on the beach. The ghosts told him to do this because the shells were dry after the years they'd stood in his house.

The ghosts told him to wait above the beach in the ferns with the geckos until the early morning light.

He did this, and when the sun first peeked above the horizon he saw the six men who'd been in his service for fifty years come down to the beach.

Each one lay in a tidepool with a turtle shell. They called to him, speaking together as though with one voice, saying they had come to his service to bring dignity to his life, because he believed that turtles should have dignity and had lived his life in that belief, even if his neighbours disapproved and scolded him.

They said they'd have another fifty years to live, because turtles lived long, and then, entering their shells, changed themselves back into sea turtles and pulled themselves down the beach with their leathery flippers and vanished into the ocean.

1592

"I have something for you, my old friend."

"Thank you, Claudio. What is it?"

I could see there was a booklet in his hand.

"Something I've done in secret. A surprise for you, Gianni."

75

"Thank you."

"I can see you are weak. Can you sit up?"

"I can," I said.

With Claudio's help, I pulled myself up to sitting. Then, leaning me forward, he fluffed up the pillows against the headboard. Even feeling so poorly, I reached my hand up and grasped his manhood, and despite himself and the occasion he responded with sudden firmness.

Then he laughed.

"You are irrepressible, Gianni!"

"I'm a little surprised at myself," I said, laughing in turn. "We don't think of ourselves as sick or dying, even when we're past forty years. We are still ourselves."

"I'm glad the fever has left your heart and spirit whole."

"Not without worries, Claudio. I worry about you. I worry about our lives together. I worry if you've been happy."

"Then you are shaken by your fever, Gianni, and nothing else. You know very well how blessed and happy I've been to live and work with you all these years. I say this now as clearly as I can, so you might hear me clearly and have no more worries about these things. Please, Gianni. About this you may have confidence."

"I believe you, Claudio, and I won't worry. But we've had to keep so much secret."

"It's been a poorly kept secret! It is our trade, and our reputation in that trade, that has protected us. As long as we made no public show of ourselves, no one had any reason to disrupt our lives. We've made no enemies."

"We've made no enemies because you are such a good man, Claudio. They love you here in Venice, they love you across the way in Murano. Even the Pope in Rome loves you."

"His Holiness sent us a book to print and publish. This doesn't mean he loves me!"

We both laughed.

"I have loved this trade. With all my heart I've loved it. I love the feel of the type. The rows of letters in a well-composed and well-tightened chase give me divine satisfaction. I love the smell of the inks and the texture of the papers. And the result — a crisp, clean, balanced blue-black impression of a page in the paper — is so much greater again than the sum of its parts."

"I have loved it too, and I've loved you for loving it. All of this has showed in the quality of work we've produced. So many fine volumes."

"It is your greatness with the Latin language that has made our reputation, Claudio. People little notice whether the letterforms are well arranged or if the ink is dark and the impressions are even on the page. They read and can see the texts have been studied and prepared by a scholar of great force. This has been our reputation."

"I will take your compliment, Gianni, only because I know you know better. We've survived these great labours by our mutual praise!"

"The public confirms our estimate of each other by their patronage. All the great families of Venice and Florence and many of Rome and elsewhere have bought our books, or have engaged us to produce books for them."

"This is most satisfying, Gianni."

"It is good to finish life with this satisfaction, Claudio."

"Do not talk of finishing life! It breaks my heart to hear it."

"You are right. I won't speak of it. But understand it is helpful for me to say so. I want to be prepared for the world to come, and unafraid. If it's not my time, there's no harm done by that effort."

"Was Brother Hilarius helpful to you today?"

"He is kind, and prayed with great fervour."

Claudio suddenly looked perplexed.

"Thinking you might be gone, now I don't know what to say. We always talk about our work, the business of the shop, and about our designs and texts and illustrations. Our plans for the future."

"What do you have for me, Claudio?"

"What?"

"You said you had something for me, that was made without my knowing."

"Yes, by the devils this past month, while you've been absent."

"What is it?"

"Now we speak of your passing, it doesn't seem as important."

"I'm glad of that, Claudio, because no crafted thing is as important as our friendship."

The tension in his face eased when I said this.

"It is a catalogue. Of all the books we have printed."

"Twenty-five years' work!" I said smiling. "Let me see."

Claudio put the booklet in my hands.

"Look at that. Imagine our printing the text of the Requiem Mass for our first broadside! What were we thinking?!"

We looked at each other, eye to eye, tears forming in each.

"This makes me happy, Claudio. This gift is the sum of my life with you. I am fortified to see it. So many pass on with no sense of achievement, in emptiness. With this, should I pass on today, it will be in fullness."

"If you do, this will be our last book. My last."

"Why, Claudio? You have three good journeymen and as many energetic devils."

"I will give Mario the shop to continue with a new imprint."

"I understand, Claudio. But don't let your life end because I am gone. That does my spirit no good. Every moment lived is a gift of God, who would surely be displeased if you scorned a single day."

"My life has taken place in you. I do not know what kind of a life it can be without you. Every day has been shared."

"I cannot tell you what to do, but rest assured I have no pleasure in leaving here without you. The best I can tell myself is that our Lord Christ promised us eternal life in the hereafter, where we will be together always in him."

"I know that's true, Gianni. But I'm afraid that God has not approved of our way of life, and that our rejoining will be in long purgatory, or worse, thereafter."

"The faith of my life has been in our Lord Christ, and it is hard for me to imagine any such thing. But if it be so, then I will stand, look St. Peter in the eye, and tell him I have lived my life faithfully, obeying what is natural to my spirit."

"And if we are still condemned, as even the Gospels declare we might be?"

"Then I will tell St. Peter I have done no evil."

"And if he says you have been fooled by the devil all along?"

"Then I will say I have loved as my own heart directed me to love, and will go to my punishment without regret or complaint."

1545

They say the eyes still see, and I discover this pained instant they do. One seconds' worth, like one frozen windowpane, my house, aflame, ahead of my gaze on the flat, damp plain of Fyn. My brain thinks as well, for I hear my fleet thoughts. How long we have lived unmolested here! To see my loving wife brutally slain, what grief and outrage fills my breast! My children, I know not. Slavery, or also death? What interest have the Franks in burning Denmark! What cowards they are! They come upon us in darkness, dragging us out in sleep and hewing off heads from horseback. What rogues they are! In the light of day — nay, merely awakened — they would weather a fierce fight, and I am strong. The Danes are strong, and brave warriors. To Asgård I go, with you wife. We go.

1506

I'm cold.

It's cold in this room.

All my life I have felt cold.

My heart was ruined between the morning and evening of a single day, when I was younger. Ruined for love. Ruined for life.

I cannot account for the tenacious effect of that failed meeting. Be assured, I have not otherwise behaved in any obsessive manner in my entire life.

What can I know is truth? Can I rely on my own thoughts? The gentle voice of my thoughts tells me I have memories of times before this time, times when some living part of me lived before. But I cannot assure myself that these are matters of any tangible truth, except in my faith in myself.

These memories have been as simple and clear in my mind as any I have known over the thirty-one years of my life in Spain. But others do not speak of any memory of any other times they have lived, so I have never spoken of it myself, in the knowledge I could be condemned to death by the Inquisitors of the Church.

It would not normally be easy for a woman to survive on her own, but after the failed encounter I travelled to the mountains in the east, having the safety of my engagement as a housemaid to a wealthy family.

I accompanied the travelling party of my mistress when she decided to relocate to her estate house in the Alps, having an ailment of breathing that the mountain air might relieve, the area also free of conflict. This has been a great age of discovery across the oceans, but also one of persistent warfare and strife.

There was another great house in the vicinity of our new alpine home, near a village where livestock and produce and other wares and services could be had. A wealthy family of Spanish Arabs lived there. They were scholars and intellectuals, whose business and livelihood was the translation of Greek and Arabic books into Latin, although they did not require the income.

Uncommon for a woman, I had a good knowledge of Latin and also some Greek. Regardless of my low status, as a maid to their neighbour, I was often welcomed into the house and joined in long and pleasant conversations about language and linguistics. My employer took an enlightened view, encouraging me to accept their invitations, knowing that my knowledge was genuine and that I had a contribution to make to these gatherings.

My mistress did not survive her affliction, a consumption of the lungs. On her passing, my Arab friends invited me to come and live at their house, which was a refuge for me, and nothing less than the preservation of my life. While plainly aware of this,

they were also generous, making it clear that joining their household did not entail me to subservient obligations but was made
in the honest friendship that had grown through our meetings and
conversations over the four years I'd lived adjacent.

I accepted on the grateful condition that I contribute fully to the
labour of maintaining the house, to which they consented, saying
I could choose whatever endeavour suited me. I said I was good at
woodworking, something also usually the province of men, but
which did not surprise them. Nor were they disappointed with the
quality of my work, which I have done diligently each day these
past six years, both cutting, fitting, and finishing, and also some
carving. I have repaired and renewed the woodwork to the interior
and exterior of the house and service buildings, and have added
ornamental work in an Arabian style.

This together with many hours spent in the garden with both
the master and his sons discussing subtleties of the Latin language
in its various forms of change over the centuries, and also its new
ecclesiastical forms, then emerging.

I have learned a good amount of Arabic in the course of that,
as you might expect, though not sufficient to make any contribution
to their scholarship. My role has been that of their study; but which,
I believe, has been mutually rewarding.

Their breadth and scholarship, together with being Islamic and
not Christian, might have encouraged me to share the secret of my
remembrances with them, but I did not dare. The refuge of their
house was vital to my living outside of slavery, and I could not
risk the possibility that anything might alienate me from their best
regard. Talking about mystical issues might have given them to
think I had become, or was becoming, imbalanced, because they
were scientific and analytical, always showing keen reason and
precision in their thinking.

Slavery was my only alternative to their refuge because I could
not have marriage. I had only one love, only one I could love, which
love I could not betray for its weight in my heart and soul.

I remembered, you see. I remembered how three centuries before
this I had formed a bond with another spirit — which means some

essence of ourselves — a promise to be together always, which by my remembrance was an inviolable pledge in my life now.

More remarkably, I saw this spirit in his present lifetime. I met the man and knew it was him.

This happened when I was young, only just a woman, at a shop in my village where I had gone to buy wine. He was there, also to buy wine. Looking into his eyes, in one explosive instant I saw our true spirits and was shocked, and also dismayed.

On no design of my own, this caught his attention, because I went faint as though ill and collapsed to the floor. He carried me outside to a public bench and opened my collar to give me air.

Opening my eyes to his again, my impression was renewed and more memories returned of more than one time together before, but with a particular event of great moment joining us, even longer before. Our spirits had been fused together by a great energy — a divine being. But this was not a divinity of Christ, rather a spirit of the earth, so it would have been a great heresy to speak of it, then to him, or later to anyone else.

Recovering my thoughts and bearing, I invited him to come to my house and join us for dinner, as an expression of my gratitude for his rescue. This was within due propriety, and he accepted.

My mind was rooted to him, with the most extraordinary focus. I could not believe or imagine that I had found him among all the multitudes of the earth; although it seemed natural to me that our spirits would seek and find each other, with the sublime and unknown power of divine forces at work in such things.

My joy and focus on him was so great that I did not think or remember for an instant that I had a suitor begging my attention. But he discovered this to be the case over dinner, when my mother boasted of her Sophia's good fortune. She was entitled to boast because the man was of good station and means.

But my companion of the ages reacted with a cooling in his eyes. Where he'd briefly had the happy thought of a prospect in me, that endeavour was suddenly closed. There is no man who'd draw swords on a chance and short acquaintance such as this, and he had already spoken of his plans to go to the Orient.

How could I tell him I had no intention of accepting the offer of my suitor? How could I tell him it was a mistake?

The urgency of the moment filled and paralyzed my mind!

I took him aside and tried to explain I had strong feelings for him, but this only reinforced the possibility I might be trouble — or flighty and impulsive — and he gently said as much in his reply.

I could not explain it was a mystic bond of ancient times that had brought us together. What lunacy that would have appeared! He had no intuition of these things, faithful only to the religion of his upbringing and to the obligations and mores of our society.

He left our house after dinner. He left for the Far East that same week and did not return to Spain. I do not know his fate.

The continuance of our lasting bond hinged on one vital hour, and I failed to make the connexion, failed to make him aware, which brought my heart to a standstill thereafter. Even to this very day, as I lie in my own sickbed of unlikely recovery. What cruel fate, that something so profound could turn on trivialities! What troubled destiny brought us to our long futures on a bootlace?!

While I pray to Christ for absolution and forgiveness, I depart from the teachings of my Church in the knowledge of my remembrances, and go in the belief that whatever carries on of the soul for him and me will be renewed again in some later place.

How I will locate him again, or he me, and how we will know each other, I do not know; except there are strong forces at work in this universe, and I pray the angelic voices will call to us both with their most compassionate guidance.

1475

I heard the arguments when I was six, nearly seven, visiting the north of India with my father.

From the time I could walk he had treated me like a man, and he took me with him on that long journey, addressing me as any other responsible man in the party. I was a child, regardless, and had some mischief in me, but this he took in good humour, joining my jokes with laughter or giving me secret signals to scold me if I were being flippant or boisterous at an inappropriate moment. But he never seemed disappointed with me. I sat with him and his travelling companions as they talked and negotiated with Indian merchants and intellectuals alike. Tibet's borders were closed to foreigners, with only a handful of Indian, Nepalese, and Chinese ever given admittance, and no Europeans. Tibetans could travel to India and China and were treated with reasonable courtesy.

"These men have not set attainable goals for themselves," he said as we left one of our meetings in India. "They will be unhappy in their lives." Then, looking me in the eye, he said, "My son, set goals for yourself that you can attain. Then attain them. As you attain them, set new goals. Then go and attain them. In this way your life is always full of reward."

When we returned from that trip, I announced to my father that I wished to enter the monastery at Sakya, a remote location in south-central Tibet. While this was a most honourable aspiration in our country, he still asked why I wanted to do this. I answered that I wanted to take the opportunity of this lifetime to clarify the direction of my lives to come.

He said he was pleasantly surprised at my answer and gave me his blessing that on my seventh birthday I could go to the gate of the monastery for the trial of admittance. He reminded me that if I passed and was taken in, neither he nor my mother could see me for five years or more.

He said if I failed and returned home in a few weeks' time, that I should feel no shame because the Abbot knew secrets about a man's inner life and would decide wisely, not on the basis of any obvious status or merit.

On my seventh birthday I went and sat at the gate of the monastery, with only my robe and bowl, also having a little tsampa and extra butter my mother had given me.

The guards shouted at me to go away, and I said I would not because I wanted to join the monastery. They threw stones and shouted ridicule at me, but I did not budge. "What do you want?" they shouted from the wall, and I said again I wanted admittance into the order. "Why do you want admittance into the order?" they shouted, but to that I was silent. "Go away!" they shouted.

I assumed the attitude of meditation and began quietly repeating a cycle of devotions, each said one hundred and eight times over, counting on my beads. My mother had shaved my head, so except that I was wearing a grey robe, I might have been mistaken for a diminutive monk already. Indeed, passers-by at the gate the following afternoon gave me alms.

When the gate was closed at evening, the monks on guard shouted at me again to go home, saying I'd be killed by bandits if I stayed outside. I said nothing but kept my back straight and eyes low, moving the beads on my rosary as the prayers and holy songs my father taught me passed my lips. The air was cold.

The next day, when the gate was open again, a monk tipped over a pot of rotten milk at my feet, which splashed on my legs and left a horrible odour around me for hours. "Go away!" they called. "You stink! Get away from here!" Later someone came up from the village with hot water and silently washed my legs and feet. I did not know who it was, except I could tell by his hands that he was a young boy like me. On the back of one hand he had a tattoo.

I passed another three days in that same spot, sitting in contemplation. Over that time I finished the tsampa my mother had given me, but others gave me alms of barley flour and butter, and one filled my bowl with hot butter tea as she passed by in the afternoon. How good it tasted! Each day after that she came and filled my bowl, and each day the guards would call and tell me to go away.

Then one morning a man jumped down from the wall with a stick and started beating me on my chest, back, and shoulders, demanding that I leave the gate. I said between blows that this violence would be upon his karma alone, that I was peaceful toward all living creatures. He was taken aback with my adult response, but preserving the fierce look on his face asked what I wanted. I said I wanted to join the order of monks in the monastery. "What do you have to give the order?" he asked, and I said only my merit, which

I give to all, as I'd also been taught, and he went away. I was sore with some bruises but tried not to be discouraged.

Early the following day, before the gate was opened, a passing sled loaded with stones drawn by a huge yak broke a rail, and all the rock was dropped on the pathway. The guards called from the wall, ridiculing me again, saying instead of sitting silent and lazy like a worthless lump, I should move the stones so people could pass into the monastery later in the day. I remembered then how the saintly Milarepa, while older than me at the time, had been called to many physical labours in his trials, so I got up and moved the pile of stones, which being a small boy took me the whole day.

When I finished at evening, several monks came up and made a fuss, saying the stones had been moved to the spot where they planned to build a new cremation vessel, asking who could have done this. I came forward and said I had, and they chastised me severely, saying I'd better move the stones to the rise further down the creek, and they'd better be moved before the Abbot came out in the morning. I worked all night and moved the stones to the rise down along the creek.

The Abbot came out the next morning, but, tired after my hours of work, I was sleeping. He shook me from sleep and kindly asked what I was doing there. I said I had been there for several days, that I'd been ridiculed, repeatedly ordered away, covered by smelly filth, beaten, and twice moved a large pile of stones. He repeated his question, asking again what I was doing there. I said I was saying prayers and mantras that my father had taught me, counting off each round of one hundred and eight with my beads.

He repeated his question a third time, and I said I wanted to come into the monastery to be his devoted acolyte. He asked me what I hoped to gain from that, and I said my father had advised me to set attainable goals, and then, when they were realized, to set new goals. My goal now was to enter the order, and when that was achieved I would set new, attainable, goals for my life there.

He asked me what those might be, and I said I did not know yet, but that they would probably be to do with clarifying the direction of my lifetimes to come. "Do you not wish to achieve Liberation in one lifetime, like the saintly Milarepa?" he asked me next, knowing that Milarepa had recently been in my thoughts.

I said that may be an attainable goal, but added how when I was in India with my father he'd been talking with Hindu and Christian holy men, who asked him why he would want to achieve release in one lifetime if the soul of the liberated was dissolved in that process. They said, wouldn't the perfected yogi wish to be perfected as the culmination of his effort? That is, to "be" in his perfection? For the Christian speakers in particular, this seemed paramount to the perfection of their yoga. They said the resurrection of the flesh after death was the distinguishing act of the yogi they followed, and seemed surprised when my father replied that every perfected yogi can perform this act. They said it is not the same if the knowledge and nature of his own being is lost as a result. I told the Abbot that to commence the path toward my Liberation, I wanted to meditate on this question and comprehend it fully.

I stopped myself, realizing I'd poured out many thoughts that I had considered with a child's understanding while I sat alone.

The Abbot then said I was unusually well-spoken for such a young boy, and how my father had given me direction both commendable and well beyond my years. He took me by the hand and walked me through the gate into the monastery.

In the twenty-eight years since, I have never been back through that gate, except once, to bring the blessing of Sanggye Menlha, or Bhaisajyaguru, the Medicine Buddha, to one of the salt men. He'd been injured and was staying at a house in the village.

Three years ago I was appointed head lama in the sacred decorative arts, with students of my own, but have now become aware that I am leaving this life into the Bardo again soon, so my tenure in this position will have been brief.

For some time after entering the order I was lonely for the company and guidance of my father and the love of my mother. The Abbot took a special interest in me but could not fully substitute for the special relationship I had with my father.

I was immediately brought to rigorous courses of study, in the knowledge of Tibetan Buddhism, called Vajrayana, or Tantricism, and its holy texts, the special teachings of our lineage, and also the language and literature of the Tibetan people.

Like the other monks, I ate two meals of tsampa and butter-tea each day, sometimes with turnip or pepper greens, and slept five hours each night on a rough blanket in my cell, which I shared with three others.

Once advanced in the fundamentals of Tibetan Buddhism and the Tibetan language, and once comfortable in the daily regimen of ritual and prayer, most monks took a special vocation. These were in a broad range of endeavour, such as debate, medicines, music or musical instrument making, sacred dance or its costume making, printing, wool making and dyeing, carpet-weaving, or the creation of sacred statues and their gilding. Others, where their talent or need dictated, worked at less refined labours, such as metal fabrication, stone cutting and building construction, woodworking, including the making of looms, the large task of cooking, or husbanding yak. Everyone worked at cleaning at appointed times. The monastery was large, having more than one thousand monks there at this time, and there were many tasks to be done. Many thousands of paces of cold stone corridors and hundreds of rooms to tidy, and thousands of butter lamps to refresh.

One day, in my fourth year at the monastery, after my eleventh birthday, early in the morning the Abbot called me to his private chamber, where after our greeting and prayers he asked me many questions. He laid objects in front of me and asked me to choose those that had appeal to me. With his permission to speak freely, I asked if he was doing this to make me a proven incarnation. He laughed, and said no, that he was already aware of my incarnations past. The next day at the same time he called me in again. This time he had several paintings hung on his wall, finely detailed sacred paintings on fabric. Again he asked me many questions, about what I saw in the paintings and my understanding of their content and composition.

I answered him as well as I could but also had the presence of mind to say that I was still a boy, and there was much I did not yet know about the worlds, gods, deities, and teachers pictured. The next morning at the same time he called for me again. This time another monk was in the room with him, who was named Brogmi in honour of one of the founders of Sakya, which founder had lived about four hundred years before. Brogmi was the head lama in the sacred decorative arts, who I succeeded three years ago. The Abbot said Brogmi was going to teach me painting. They had a painters' kit of brushes and pigments in a wooden box, which they gave to me. I prostrated myself and said many prayers, thanking them for their benevolence, trust, and kindness to me, and for their generosity in handing me such valuable tools without proof of my worthiness. After I was finished, and after they had responded with their own devotions, the Abbot said I had proved my worthiness to his satis-faction in our two previous interviews.

Brogmi had been to visit China twice in his lifetime. Since the end of the Yuan Dynasty, about one hundred years ago, there had been cordial relations between the rulers of Tibet and the Ming Emperors, and many Tibetans had taken missions to China.

Brogmi was greatly influenced by the Chinese painting he saw and brought many of these influences to the sacred art he created for Sakya, beginning to distinguish the quality of the art produced at our order from that of other Tibetan religious communities.

The first Tibetan painters before us took mostly from Indian influences and repeated the styles of Indian painters. This tradition was rigid and symmetrical. The main divinity would be portrayed in the very centre in a large scale, above which would be a supreme Buddha figure, from whom the divinity was an emanation, and above that a uniform row of lamas and teachers through whom that ritual had passed.

Later a native Tibetan custom emerged. The central divinity was replaced by a revered lama, as the manifestation of the supreme divinity, who would be pictured above him, signaled by gestures of the hands and the implements he would be given to hold.

The influence of Chinese painters brought Brogmi to be less diagrammatic than this, giving his figures a freer position, balanced by the weight, colour, and arrangement of the groups of figures as a whole. I followed him in this manner, adding further departures in my own work, such as sky and landscape motifs highlighting the main figures.

I worked hard. I began with painting the solid colours to the walls of the chapels and corridors, gradually learning to paint decorative figures. As the years went by, I progressed to painting detailed fabric hangings and then to giant temple banners.

I have seen the boy who cleaned the spoiled milk off my feet and legs as I first sat outside the monastery gate every year since that day. I recognized him by the tattoo on his hand, although he never identified himself as having helped me, nor sought any favour in return. But every year we have briefly met and exchanged a few words. Once, when he was ill, I went out to the village to see him, bringing medicinal herbs to heal him.

He was the child of a salt man and became a salt man himself when he grew up. The salt men are nomads who make the long journey with their yak to the salt lakes in northeastern Tibet each year, where, by secret methods and speaking a secret language, they gather the salt. Over the rest of the year they wander the land, trading their salt for food and other goods.

Our friendship is a curious one, returning to see one another at intervals in this way, as though moved by a larger destiny.

Our friendship has taught me things. I learned from him that our lives are made up of things we choose, and others not chosen.

Choices are the active part of living, which determine the nature and quality of our inner life, which become the quality of our lives as a whole. The things not chosen we adjust to, of necessity. Even if they are hardships, we come to value them in our way of life.

The lives of the salt men are principally hardship. They live in the barrens, with scarce resources, having few possessions. They travel long distances in cold weather for the labour of gathering a good which is neither pleasant, nor attractive, nor in itself nourishing. They do not choose this hard life, but they would not choose to leave it. It is the life they have learned how to negotiate, which brings them happiness in it.

But they have few choices in its living. You, for instance, may have the choice of meat or fish or eggs when you eat. The salt men have no such choices. Each day they eat barley dumpling broth and butter tea. They have no other choices, as their yak have no choice other than the thin mountain grass. But in other choices they are the same as you and me. They choose between anger and compassion, between decency and violence, and abidingly between strengths and weaknesses.

We each struggle to gather enough dung to burn to keep us warm. We choose to burn dung. Choose to live. Some in my order have learned the yoga of psychic heat and do not need to burn dung to stay warm. They have chosen to transcend the common experience of living in the world. Some others choose to end their opportunity as a result of oppression or despair. They are doomed to long trials in the Bardo, and hellish worlds, which most do not escape for a very long time. Perfected yogis also choose to end their experience after a time, but in their passage through the Bardo they are blessed to go to heavenly worlds. Still others might perform a courageous deed and lose their own life suddenly in that virtue.

The Buddha said that some are reborn in hell, some again in this world, and some in heaven; but the pure are not reborn. It is not the action but the intention that bears the revelation.

I wonder how it is that things arise and pass away? Why do we go forward under the threat of hells and heavens? Is it obtuse if I take risks and make mistakes in living my lives, provided I do not form attachments to what I encounter?

These are the same ideas I expressed to the Abbot when he first brought me into the monastery. I contemplate them still; and, while I comprehend that *all* things are ultimately empty — both samsara and nirvana — about the living of life, I could have some sympathy for the Hindu philosopher I heard in India as a child with my father.

I have sat on the roof of the main chapel to write these thoughts. Below me, I can see a young boy sitting outside the gate. He has been there for eight days, and the gatekeepers shout at him to go away, pelting him with little stones from time to time.

He had been sitting with another boy until the night before last, when the other was killed by bandits for a beautiful lapis lazuli bead necklace he wore as a rosary, no doubt the well-wishing gift of a loving relative. The soldiers of the monastery rushed to help him but were too late, both to save him and to apprehend the bandits, who had already raced away on their ponies.

1440

When I was young, my father told me that Sergio would marry a daughter of the Giulianos. He joked and said how, if they had no daughter, Sergio would be given to a marble statue in their garden, if that's what it took to marry him to a Giuliano.

But I *loved* him, I protested. My father said love had little force in such matters. These marriages were political contracts.

I asked him if I would be married against my will, for a political alliance. He said that, being the youngest of four girls, this was unlikely. Meaning, the first two or three would cement any needed family partnerships, and, provided it was to a good family, I would be free — or more-or-less free — to fall in love as I might.

At first, I had the impression that only women were bound by Holy law to remain faithful in a loveless marriage, while men could cavort about as they pleased with any unmarried woman they could interest.

I realize now that this was true in part, but only in part. Also, that betrothed women do the same at times, with married and unmarried men alike.

For my own part, I could not abide the risk to my eternal soul.

Many in my country, both men and women, are pious about mortal sin. As a people, this rule of law is strong in our minds. Outside Italy I do not know. I am told the lands outside Europe are mostly populated with heathens and barbarians.

In those same conversations — for I brought it up with him more than once — my father would console me, saying I should take comfort I didn't have to worry about being given to a Tartar king, or an emperor of the Chinese. At least his daughters were being given to estates in Florence.

I was acquainted with Sergio from a young age. Our families entertained together, and the children would be brought and left in the care of the host's nannies, whomever might be visiting whom. Both Sergio and his older brother were friendly toward me and would join me in games. We also saw each other at Mass, although our rules of behaviour were more formal there.

As we grew older, we had other outings. Sergio and his brother often invited one or two of my sisters and me for a boat ride, with his father or mother coming as chaperone.

Sergio's brother knew I was in love. He was in love with Isabella, my next older sister, and once come to a suitable age they were married. Being older, they were married first, before Sergio and before me. The contract between our families — the contract I needed for my happiness — was cemented by them.

I was married later to another family, to a man I do not love.

No — in truth, I love my husband well enough. But I love Sergio better. So very, very much better.

It was a cruel fate to have to attend each other's weddings. His came first, and mine followed about six months later. I was jealous and angry at his, then resentful and detached at mine. Both sins I confessed, but my heart was not relieved for that gesture.

At four years of age, his son has died today.

He was drowned, in front of my very eyes. A tragic accident.

My heart is full of guilt because I did not feel remorse for the tragic death of the small child. Instead, I had shameful gladness that Sergio would lose what he and I should have had together, instead of them. Together with the cruel hope the tragedy would bring tension and division to their marriage.

As though he was to blame for my sorrow, for not having him for my own. As though his wife had done me evil by entering the marriage arranged for them. As though I could accept his offer now, were it his wife killed in the fountain today instead of their son.

You see, my own time is short with illness now. Having lived so righteous of heart, how could I endanger my eternal soul so close

93

to the end? These hateful thoughts were inflamed in my mind, like the very fires of hell they drew upon me.

God forgive me, this was only the outburst of my long sorrows, tortured by my long — my life-long — devotion to him, never once knowing a single hour held in his loving arms, never once to hear him whisper warm words of affection in my ear.

1410

They call me the witch. The witch of the long road. The witch of the west land.

To earn this, I have not done magic anyone could know about, nor bitten the heads off chickens or rats, nor worn black robes, nor pranced unclothed in the light of the crescent moon.

I am just an old woman, living alone. I've lived and looked after myself alone on this road all of my life. I was born on this road and survived by the care of my mother until she died of fever in my fourteenth year. My father did not deny his title to me, but he did not stay with us either. Instead, he travelled the road with his goods each way, months at a time.

When he passed our tent again, he would stop and leave fabrics and money for us. He did this for a long time, even after mother passed away. Until the year came that he never went by this place again, when I was gone twenty years. I cannot know if he fell to illness, or settled in Europe with his greatness and riches, or was slain for them by thieves on the road.

You may say I am not old; but for this life, in this place, with its many dangers and few to forgive, at past forty-five years I am.

To passers-by, I have looked old all my life. This has not come from the passing years, but from living in a weathered condition. My life has been lived out-of-doors, save nights asleep in my tent, all my hours in the sun and wind. In the blown dust and debris of this road, the trade route you know as the Silk Road.

An old woman alone — strong and weather-worn in a hostile place and time — will form in peoples' minds as a witch. Travellers will call her by that name, not knowing what they say.

At least here that name doesn't come with the hate and treachery it does elsewhere, where an angry mob might have dragged me away for hanging or to be burned alive.

Here passers-by enjoy that imagining on their journey. Their fates are uncertain, and they beg a little magic to steel their hearts or an oracle to assure their worried minds. I might better be called a fortune teller, which many have said of me.

It is both by choice, and not by choice, that I have stayed here alone after the death of my mother.

It is by choice, because I have done so.

It is not by choice, because I knew no other life. Or, what is the same thing, this was the only life I knew how to live. I am not ugly or deformed, but neither have I the natural charm or beauty to sway a traveller to a proposal, much less move a man's heart to love, nor have any wealth or estate to recommend me.

So my choice was to keep a peaceful heart with what I had, where I've had it. Any foolish thinking beyond that, any childish wishes, would only have made my heart sore.

While I've said all this, I did not start out to tell you my own story, rather his. I know who you are, reading this, and I know what this story is about: and that is, him and me.

Me, I am dying soon, and will be gone. He lives still and will live another score of years.

He is a big dumb brute, a giant of a man.

He couldn't help that he had hardly more spark in his brain than you'd have rubbing two damp twigs together. At heart he was kindly, always in earnest.

Angus is in China now, where for near twelve years he has been the executioner at court for the Emperor. The tales I hear back down the road tell of a giant that everyone fears, while in genuine respect, who is known for his great strength and his sense of justice.

He was born and lived in Scotland — in the Grampians is all I know — under the rule of David, a Bruce. The Scots towered over their neighbours, the Picts, that people near-vanished since the time of MacAlpine five hundred years before, but were every bit as barbaric. They dressed with nought but a rough woven cloth wound about them, and went their way with bare arms, legs, and feet. Primitives, of raw strength and raw thought, loyal, and quick to fight, preferring to eat foods men elsewhere wouldn't give to hogs.

Angus found himself in difficulty at the time of the occupation of the French under the Admiral Jean de Vienne, and he needed to escape from Scotland, else he believed he would be hunted by the French until they saw him dead.

Angus made his way to Aberdeen, where he found a ship of Moroccans at harbour, who were traders. He stole aboard at night and asked them if he could travel with them, to whatever port they may be bound.

They said he could and took him below deck, where they sat him to a great oar and shackled one leg. There were thirteen others also at oar, some European, some Mediterranean, some African.

The great daft dunce hadn't the blessing of inspiration he'd been taken prisoner. He sustained the belief he was working for passage, with no other thought about it. He rowed, they brought him food. He'd known a harder life than that before.

They travelled far abroad.

The giant grew ever stronger for his well-fed long days' work, hour upon hour pulling his oar, 'til his arms — already of great power — were like tree-trunks in their bulk.

They went down the Atlantic coast of France to Portugal. Then through the pillars and up along the south coast of Spain, across to the Barbary Coast, then to Palestine. Weeks went by.

There in Palestine the thought passed the mind of Angus that he was out from under the threat of his French pursuers, and there in the orient (as he called it) he could go his way freely. As they sat idle in port, he said as much to the gangman.

This same gangman thought the whole idea to be hilarity and laughed and spat on the great dumb Scot, his prisoner at oar.

This latter gesture was a great mistake for the gangman, as it brought an anger to Angus's naïve and loyal mind, who'd thought himself working for food and transport, which he'd done with utmost diligence. The candle was suddenly lit in his skull that he was a prisoner, as the Moroccans conceived it anyway, and more-over that these were men who'd soil his dignity on a trifle.

He stood up suddenly. Like blind Samson bringing down the temple, in a swelling rage he tore the chains from their mounting rings with his bare hands, freeing his fellow slaves in doing so. As they escaped, he wrapped the chain around the gangman's head and throat and left him senseless, tied in iron.

Next Angus pulled down a great beam, a support for the deck planks above. He pounded that beam on the hull under his feet like he were churning butter, until he broke clear through, shattering the span of a yard of lumber. The seas poured in.

Angus hadn't made a plan in his rage, nor had he contemplated his escape. As the water swelled 'round his waist, he still hadn't given it thought. But he heard a voice call in his ear. Nay, which seemed to've laid hold and pulled him along by the ear.

"This way! This way!" the tiny voice said.

Angus thought it must be an angel.

He was not far off the truth but of a different mystic canon. It was a sprite that had been with him invisible since Scotland to look over him on his way through foreign lands, and had revealed herself only as this crisis had arisen.

"This way!" she said, pulling him by the earlobe.

While she pulled him out into the water with one hand, she reached into her little bag with another and sprinkled them both with dust to make them invisible. She well knew that such a large man, with his beacon of flaming red hair, could scarcely escape attention once they got onto the shore and into the town.

The shore was only a few minutes' swim for our Goliath. He came up on land hardly wanting for breath but curious indeed about who his rescuer had been. His gentle mind was much in awe when they stood wet on the sand and he could see the sprite floating in front of him, the two invisible to all else and others.

In this invisible state they made their way out of the port city. They did not know their way, but they could see the great caravans being loaded with goods for India and China and could hear the bearers talking about their journey ahead.

They followed the path of the caravans and thereby followed the road. They were soon safe from the Moroccans, who were dispersed after the loss of their vessel and were not equipped to follow him for vengeance. Besides, only the gangman knew any part of what had actually happened, and he did not survive the sinking.

So it was not long before the sprite brought the Scot to bathe and shed his cloak of invisibility.

On the road, all were afraid of the man for his great size and barbaric dress and appearance, and his reputation spread.

I heard about the red-haired giant many days before he passed this way. None dared challenge him, and he was said to frequently defend the wretched. He was given a sword by an Indian he rescued from treachery at the hands of bandits, which he always wore thereafter, increasing everyone's apprehension of him.

I did not know it was him until I actually saw his person. In that moment I had a revelation and was deeply amazed.

I could see the sprite, who was surprised at my seeing, but accepting and unafraid.

"Do you know this Scot and I have an ancient connexion and bond in the mystic?" I asked her.

"I do," she replied.

"Will you bid him stay over in this place?" I asked her. "For a few weeks, together again."

"I will," she replied.

1364

It is within my long lifetime that I have seen Tibet again restored to its glory and independence.

After nearly a century of domination, the power of the Mongols began to slip fifteen years before my birth with the death of Kublai.

Their hierarchy had its government in Saskya, and as the Yuan dynasty declined so did its remote viceroys after the death of the mighty Kublai's successor Timur, when I was in my twenty-seventh year, or 1307 by the European calendar.

I know the European calendar on account of my life of constant travel with my husband and child, from Tibet out to foreign lands and back and out again, for the buying and selling of goods abundant in one country in exchange for those scarce in the other.

There was much destruction of lives and property in the course of our struggle to free ourselves of the invaders.

When I was fifteen years old, for instance, the great monastery of Bri-kung was destroyed in battle with the Mongols, with the death of many fighting monks.

It wasn't until I was fifty-two years old that our leader emerged, who could form a Tibetan kingship, eventually ousting the foreigners. His name was Byang-chub Gyal-mtshan. In his long struggle for Tibet he suffered torture, treachery, ridicule, and imprisonment; but eventually, only ten years ago, he was finally victorious over our enemies and established a new monarchy in the same city where the Mongols had sat.

Since then, he has endeavoured to remove all traces of Mongol influence in Tibet, gradually elevating his title through Ruler, Divine Lord, and recently Most High. He has revised the taxes under which we have suffered, built new bridges and border posts, and rediscovered the Fivefold Set of Scrolls — books telling of the achievements of the ancient kings, and how the demons of Tibet were quelled by the power of the new Buddhist law.

I am so happy to have lived through this transformation and to have seen so much of my country with my own eyes, trod under my own feet.

The greatest privilege of all, my husband and I went to Mount Kailas, about which we made a slow pilgrimage, advancing prostrated on our hands and knees the entire way, wooden blocks tied to our palms to preserve the skin of our hands as we went, and wearing stiff aprons for our knees. Together we repeated our invocations as we went.

Our trading took us thrice to China, but, while the Mongol lords were as little popular with the native Chinese, this remained an inauspicious destination. They had little interest in our Tibetan goods in China, and on our return we found there was a stigma upon Chinese goods brought back to my country.

The Indian provinces, Nepal, and the smaller kingdoms nearby them in the Himalayas were better destinations, whether Buddhist, Hindu or, while rare, Christian or Muslim communities. We were received respectfully and established trustworthy relationships with many traders in these regions. They were happy with the goods we brought to them, and we could usually negotiate mutually fair values in exchange for their domestic product.

I am amazed I have lived so long, to an age not often achieved in this country. I credit the regular exercise of our travels, the love of my husband, and the varied diet I have enjoyed.

Regardless, I expect to journey to a new continuation again soon, a traveller on a known but unremembered road. I heard once that the hidden books, the *gter ma*, of the great Padma Sambhava include a liberation by hearing for the intermediate state; but, if so, his incarnation as *Tertön* to take out this folio has yet to appear. Perhaps he is born and a youth in this world even as I write these words.

I wonder where I shall go? Wherever it is, I should like to stay put next time, while others wear down their shoes out my window.

We have had so little hardship, my husband and myself. Oh, we have worked hard and throughout our lives have always worked. But that is not hardship. We have been prosperous for our labour and have escaped mortal peril along the way, whether illness, accident, warfare, or natural calamity. We are like one person, and I wonder if our paths are further knit in the future.

Our daughter has had some hardship in Tibet, being of Hindu parentage, finding many reluctant to accept her as the child of Tibetan parents. Instead she was regarded as a foundling in Tibetan care. She was given us by an Indian woman of our old acquaintance, who could not keep her.

This lack of acceptance never roused her to anger, and she has handled her sorrow with calm and dignity. She has found much greater acceptance now in Gyal-tse, where we have lived these past six years since our retirement from trading.

Our daughter, whom we named for the sister of Milarepa, is an authority on medicinal herbs. She gained this talent over our many years of travel through the mountains, where she gathered small plants every day as we walked, studying them and learning their properties. She gained much knowledge through the teachings of experts both in Tibet and in India, where she always found them intrigued to meet a young woman interested in their calling. She formed many close alliances, and it was not many years before other of these experts were, in genuine modesty, asking her counsel on issues.

She can now earn a good living with her knowledge, as she knows the healing properties of plants and is often generously rewarded, when for instance she might add years to the life of a wealthy man, or the wife or child of a wealthy man.

She never asks for payment but always receives it from those able to pay. But never asking for payment means she can equally accept the poor and also those who've turned away from worldly possessions, relieving their physical ills where it is natural and good to do so.

When I spoke of the mortal peril my husband and I have escaped, I neglected to say how our daughter frequently brought us relief, which untreated would have escalated in others to their passing.

But I have asked her to extend no treatment to us now, no matter how profound her love for her adopted father and mother. The time has come when we return ourselves to the divine.

1280

I have put my thoughts into a painting. My painting has been a great labour. It has taken more than one year to complete. I am grateful to have had the time and leisure needed to create this painting.

Each step required to complete this work has been painstaking.

I began with the idea of putting my thoughts into images.

I asked myself, How do I capture the essence of the experience of my life?

That essence has not been to do with the politics and warfare of men, or the Henry kings, or glorious Alexander king away in Scotland, or old Arthur king, or any other, nor their bows and catapults and brave knights, nor even the churches and priests subject in their domains. Here in the west of Dumnonia, or Cornovii by its old Roman name, lately Cornwall to the Britons, we have been subject to these British for gone three centuries. Cornwall was made an Earldom of Wessex under King Athelstan, who killed the last Cornish king in the year 936.

It has only been in a church that I have seen another painting, besides my own. The possibility of recording thoughts into eternity with pigments on board did not occur to me until seeing this other painting on display in the church.

That was a telling and moving moment in my life, to discover that such a thing existed. I have learned something about the world and its geography over my years, with some small grasp of its scale, also its peoples, and of Cornwall and its peoples in relation to other lands and peoples, but I am in no way worldly. I have not travelled to see other lands and peoples, what they have built, what crops they raise, or what animals they husband.

I'm keenly aware how fortunate I've been to have lived a sheltered life here in our wood in the southeast of Cornwall, hidden from the violence and intrigue of the men of this era. We've kept ourselves hidden, keeping a small farm on a sloped clearing in the wood, nearby some stones left by the ancients, growing greens and berries, keeping some chickens and pigs, and hunting wild birds for meat from time to time. I have sometimes wished for adventure over the seas in foreign lands, but only in rare flights of fancy.

We escaped here as children, at about thirteen years of age, brought together by the death of both of our fathers, who were fighting men, on the same day at the port of Looe, whereafter our mothers were taken away. I was found by a friar of a monastery nearby the town, who brought me far away to this wood and left me here, and still returns to visit from time to time.

My companion came by his own devices on foot, a young boy alone in a dangerous land, arriving at this neglected haven somewhat by chance.

The priestess said it was not by chance at all, but providence.

On this, there were questions that arose in my mind when I planned and contemplated my painting.

How could I communicate the significance of the companion in my life and how uniquely close we have been?

How could I possibly describe the events the day the mist bridge appeared in the clearing?

Both of these things are so much larger than language, even the subtle words of our native Cornish.

Cornish is a Brythonic tongue, with Welsh and Breton. These were the southern languages of the Britons, Manx and Gaelic the northern. I was taught these things by my friends at the monastery. My good friends, to whom I owe a great debt.

My questions were not only larger than language but larger than a painting also, even a very large painting like mine. It is as tall as my companion and half as wide as it is tall.

I made the board on which it's painted from oak planks, smoothing the edges with a drawblade, joining them with dowels, then pasted together with glue boiled from animal bone. Then I carefully worked its surface with a drawblade until it was smooth. Next I sealed the surface with a gesso of gelatin, boiled from animal sinews to a thin paste. On that I added a base from the white of chicken eggs, boiled in water with oil crushed from sunflower seeds. When this had dried, my friend helped me prop the prepared painting board up against the wall, and I was ready to begin.

You will wonder how I gained knowledge of the methods of painting, having never painted before, and I will answer that I sought the advice of the learned brothers at the monastery who had knowledge of these things, and much was given to experiment.

Other insights, bearing more on inspiration than skill, I gained when the Divine joined into me.

There are two other women with whom she joined at the same moment, as she flew into her three aspects, which could not join in one mortal soul.

Birth. Death. Beauty.

The others were immediately gone from me that day, gone away to their own long careers.

I created the paint colours for my work depending on the needs of the portion I was painting. The paints were all temperas, made by mixing the whites of chicken eggs with water and pigments.

The pigments I gathered from many sources, including earths, tarnished metals, green plants, flowers, and berries, among others. I needed many colours for my painting.

It was my companion and lover for the ages who suggested the manner in which I might capture the events of my life into one large painting.

We were walking in the wood together, and I was talking about this question, saying, Should I paint you and me together? Should I paint the mist bridge? The Divine crossing to see us?

He did not answer but instead bent and plucked me a dog rose, which I took from his hand.

I continued asking, saying, How would I convey the enjoyment we had together as children, before she came?

He smiled, and I knew my asking these questions was not an annoyance but instead a pleasant recollection. He bent and plucked a tall spire of foxglove, with brown-bronze coloured blossoms stacked down like tiers of little drinking horns.

I realized then there was meaning by handing me the digitalis, that many events were associated in my mind with the wildflowers of our beloved Cornwall. I would paint my life in flowers, even if the message of the flowers was private to myself or shared only with my companion.

For my birth it was common vetch, for which I needed red-hued pigments for its delicate round blossom, perched on long brownish stems with pairs of skinny leaves at even intervals up them, like so many oars out each side of a longboat, and with curly ends at the tips, past the rows of leaves. The vine was used for green fodder.

For reasons unknown to me, my mother kept a dried vetch blossom in my birth locket.

For my life on the Lizard coast as a young child it was stinking iris, not on account of any unpleasant associations there, but that they were plentiful on the wetlands property we kept house beside, for which I needed a blend of yellows into pinks and white.

Have it go without saying that the colours I describe were for the blossoms, the leaves and stems for most all being shades of green. Except sometimes the stems, as with the vetch already mentioned, and willowherb, which also has a brownish stem.

I painted willowherb in remembrance of the friar kindly taking me away from Looe.

Their small, pale purple flowers were out the day we first travelled northwest toward this wood, where he knew I could be hidden and would be safe, and that his monastery was not a great distance away so he could return and check on my health and safety, which he did with great caring and diligence. It is called willowherb because its leaves resemble those of a willow tree.

Also on our way, as we sneaked through little-travelled paths, and also with a brownish stem, was bog pimpernel, spreading wide where it grew with many small green leaves. Its stems are punctuated with small, five-peaked flowers, standing tall and away from the leaves on their own stems from the vine, looking like the red underside of a starfish when the blossom is open.

For my first night in the wood I painted field poppy, which greeted me in the clearing where we made a shelter of dead branches and vines for me to sleep in the open, where I would be troubled by fewer shadows until I was comfortable in this place. There were dozens of poppies out the front opening of my new home, their broad beacon-red, black-dotted faces waving at me on skinny tall stems rough with hairs.

The friar brought me food for the first while, but I soon had to learn to gather and grow my own. For my first recollection of this I mixed white pigment with a hint of pink for the tiny star blossom of blackberry, although which flowers had already passed on my arrival at the wood, to provide me with succulent berries. I had to defend a patch of blackberry I claimed for my own from birds, who also enjoyed its tasty abundance. I wove a fine netting from spent vines to protect some for myself until the berries were fully ripe, when they fall into your hand on the slightest bump, but not so ripe they have fallen themselves to the ground, where I would leave them for rodents.

Next I painted common violet, mixing the colour from pink magenta and leaving a light of the same in the six petals of its purple flowers, with a small button of yellow at the centre, standing above round leaves. These violets were in remembrance of the sloped clearing in the wood to the east of where I stayed the first while, nearby the old stones.

So important was the next flower I painted, I made a pattern of them around other of the flowers in my painting. These were evening primrose, which grows tall and strong in many areas of our wood. I first saw my companion among evening primrose, at night. I carried a torch, and he was hidden, but I could see his eyes reflecting the light among many yellow primrose flowers, which blossoms open in darkness. I was greatly startled, fearing in the first instant it was a wild animal, like a badger, which could do me harm. But I'd seen badgers before and knew they were shy of fire, so I would be safe with the torch. But in another instant I realized it was human and not animal, and then was afraid it might be a soldier or a bandit who would do me harm. But I thought how this person was hiding, whereas a solider would be bold and without fear of me. So I spoke and asked who it was, and he said he was only a boy who had lost his father in the fighting at Looe. I answered him that I was also alone and was a girl who had also lost her father in that fighting.

We became friends straight away, and before long the next day had pledged to keep each other safe forever.

He was a friendly boy, always lively and cheerful. The friar also took him into his care, coming to see us about once each fortnight. He did this on condition that we not be lovers, even as we lie and sleep together, until our sixteenth year had passed and we'd become better aware of our bodies and could care for any consequences of our union. When he first came we were neither of our maturity yet, so had no difficulty consenting, not knowing what he meant exactly. But we kept our word to the friar regardless, and all our mutual esteem was rewarded for it.

We started to build a little house in the clearing near the ancient stones, in which remembrance I painted honeysuckle. For this I mixed pink sienna and yellows for its small, sprawling blossoms crowded on the brown stems of the shrub. It grew on one side of the wood, where we found fallen timber ideal to cut into planks and boards for our house. This cutting was made easier by the loan of a longsaw from the holy brothers, and sometimes their help if they were in need of the physical exertion, which they sometimes lacked in their devotions and could be found in the liberty of visiting us.

Columbine they say is like a cluster of five doves. I had trouble finding tints to colour my tempera its blue-purple but eventually made it mixing the juices of berries, which I dried on stones. I painted columbine because it reminded me of when we added live-stock to our assets. These had to be bought, and all we could do for money at the time was cut wood, so we cut many planks and boards and square timbers over weeks and weeks and sold them through the pious brothers for coins to buy animals. We sold them in this arrangement as it enhanced their reputation as a useful enterprise with their landlord — the monastery was on a managed estate for its protection — and ensured secrecy for us. When we went to buy the livestock, two pigs and six chickens, there was columbine nearby the gate of the yard where we collected them. To the breeders we were only nameless, faceless youths with silver to buy the pigs and chickens, so we did not worry for our anonymity.

Later we grew mustard to sell, seeding a wild charlock, which happy large yellow blossoms I also painted.

You will be starting to wonder how I fit so many flowers into my picture, but I said the board was large, and I painted to life-size, usually in a small sample. Even so, there were more wildflowers than these in and around our wood. And many more memories.

We worked hard, but I do not mainly remember the labour. I mainly remember the play, the joy we had. We worked hard and we played like children. He especially loved to play hide-and-seek.

I painted daffodil recalling our hide-and-seek games, six broad yellow petals behind a fluted yellow bowl, on thick stems with wide green leaves. Once in the spring when the bulbs were at their height he hid in daffodils, and when I found him at last we lay there and breathed them in while he held me close.

Our lives were full, and we did not feel lonely for the company of others. Once we were established, the friar would usually bring others from the monastery on his fortnightly visit that he knew he could trust. We would often make a large fire and sit through the night, toasting vegetables and joking and talking. Once they brought sugar treacle and butter and we made a caramel, which we dripped and let harden. You had to be careful not to bite it in your mouth, but reduce it with your tongue instead, or it could easily stick at risk of pulling a tooth free.

We also talked of religion and belief, but about these matters I would always say I would have to resolve them at some future time, and they would laugh.

We had greater celandine by our house. The sight of its four large yellow petals indeed heralded the return of the swallows, as they say. We had many birds and were friendly with all. They trusted us and were not nervous around us. We saved seeds and drippings and what else we could find to encourage them to come to our house.

For some years there was a hedgehog who lived on the path to the spring that would come out and nibble my heels when I stopped to rest — at least that was the feeling of it. I stopped there to pull up the roots of red valerian, which I used to make a soothing tea for us when the work was hard. I painted the flower, which is more pink than red with many small flowers in clumps (entirely different from the white variety) in memory of those rest stops, when I would be greeted by my shy little woodland friend.

Thinking of those called "red" that were more like pink, we had red campion, which I painted. My thoughts of this flower were for the joy I had in my friend, the inexhaustible good spirits he brought to my life, and the smiles and laughter we shared. Even when some misfortune brought us gloom, his strong spirit would patiently rally against it.

When it was first out in its robust glory, I would bring red campion home and wind it into a garland like the ancients did for their
athletic contests. When my hero came home from farming our gar-
dens, I would greet him on the porch and bid him down on one
knee, where I would give him the garland on his head. He would
rise, gently waving his arms as though greeting a crowd of cheering
admirers, then flex the muscles of his arms to show how much he
deserved an athletic award. My heart would burst with love for him
then, no matter how many seasons we repeated this comic charade.

For our garden plot, he moved many marsh marigolds to the edges
because these flowers discouraged a number of destructive insects,
leaving more of its vegetables for the gardeners. I painted ruffled
deep-yellow marigolds in my grateful thoughts of the abundance of
our garden, although it took several years to collect and build a
supply of seeds for a good variety of nourishing plants. We also had
many berries, which were mostly wild, but which we concentrated
in areas to grow by dropping seed berries on the ground, left under
leaves, or partially buried in damp soil to encourage them to ger-
minate in something of a garden area for us.

Another I dearly loved, which I painted — although we didn't
have them right nearby, they could be found in the ancient hedgerows just outside the wood — was blackthorn. Its burst of white
flower was glorious and sublime in the spring. Its sloe berry made
a hard liquor, which I did not like to drink, but its wood, pruned
to grow as a tree rather than entwined in hedgerows, was of a most
satisfying quality to handle and made an excellent walking stick.
The friars said some of the blackthorn hedges had existed in
Cornwall as we saw them there for two thousand years or more,
planted by the most primitive of the ancients.

Southeast of the stones was a place where white Cornish clay
could be found. We did not have the machinery to blast this fine
clay into pottery; but if we gathered it, one of the holy brothers
had a cousin in a distant town who was employed at this craft
and would exchange finished pots and plates for weights of clay.
Meadow buttercup grew on the way there, in which recollection I
added that flower to my painting.

We traded for fabric to make clothing, which I would dye and sew myself. We had to have shoes as well, which we bought from a travelling merchant. This was one of the few things for which we needed money, though once acquainted with the merchant, who came to the feudal peasant's village on the same estate as the monastery, which is the property of an Earl of King Henry, he would accept other goods in trade.

We saw the Earl pass in his carriage on the highway once, as we were returning home with great weights of white potting clay on our backs, but we never saw his castle, which you may call a great house instead, though understand it was impressive. We were already well-disposed to the Earl, for the excellent good treatment and support he gave to the monastery, and the brothers said he was a devout man while also a brave warrior.

He must have been in a reflective mood that day on the highway because they were passing slowly, and when he saw us with the great weight on our backs, I could hear him say to another man with him in the carriage, "See these rustics, how hard they labour! Yet the entitlement for their honest hard work is so little, while so many dishonest men amass great fortunes with no labour at all." With that he drew his purse and threw us each a gold sovereign — each worth more than an ordinary seaman would earn in three years or more. We saved these coins and their value remained true, indeed it increased, until in recent years that value has afforded us some rest because our health has not been as good.

There is a bog on the other side of the wood from the old stones, to the southwest, where there was some thick natural peat. There was not much available to harvest, and we did not want to scar the land either, so we kept only small amounts dried for use as fuel in emergency, if we had trouble finding fallen dry sticks for a faggot. We would not cut trees for fuel for heating or cooking unless it were damaged beyond recovery from illness, insects, or lightning.

In memory of our journeys to the bog for peat, I painted common butterwort, which grew there. With its violet-like flowers, I was always fascinated with this plant because of its diet of insects, which it would trap inside with sticky stuff excreted from its fleshy leaves.

We were so fortunate, as I mention lightning. Three times over the years there was fire in the wood from lightning, but none that spread nor came close to threatening our house.

We were not so fortunate in the wake of the friar's blessing for the consequences of our union. We wanted to have children, and tried to have children when we were young, and I was with child once. But it was stillborn, and after that I was barren. Often in my dreams I was with child but never in the living world.

My life of dreams was rich, about which I felt fortunate, and about which I painted shamrock leaves. You may find it amusing, but when I reflected upon it I was always grateful. Dreaming so richly and so frequently seemed to make my life larger, as though my living years were doubled. Others passed their nights mostly in sleep, only counting their time in days, but I passed long nights — while having my rest — in varied landscapes far away, many I know to be in the future, both the near future and the distant future.

This plentiful dreamworld was a result of my merger made with the divine, I think. About this I have already said obliquely but not described in any direct way. In truth, I don't know how, and think you will be skeptical reading of it. We could call it a dream. That you could accept because your own dreams are fantastic.

In this dream, my companion and I were in the meadow where the old stones stand, in late summer two years after our first coming to the wood, when our home and our first garden were established.

We slept in the open in the meadow that night, under the bright stars. I always paid close attention to the stars and could point out many significant things as we lay, and knew the locations of the planets as they made their long slow transits.

Early in the morning, when we awoke, the landscape in the meadow had changed. There was a bridge coming out of the fog — for it was more than mist — over the trees to the ground near where we'd slept. It was greenish in colour, and nearly transparent, but bore our weight when we took a step onto it.

When we did, the Great Goddess came out of the haze, over the mist bridge, on foot. She spoke to us, saying she existed in a divine state, but that the whole world would not be elevated to that same divinity until she had rejoined the corporeal, and, through many transformations, perfected her divinity again out of that condition.

She asked if she might live in me. A genuine question, meaning I could have declined. I did not wish to decline, and I looked at my companion for his approval. He nodded lovingly, so I replied to her that she could.

Two other women were there in the meadow with us suddenly, whom the Goddess said she had brought magically, and who had consented to receive her other aspects.

Her radiance grew suddenly, and she became like pure energy, rapidly flowing into each of us, with my companion affected as well, though not receiving the Goddess.

What you will find difficult to comprehend is that there was an intermediate step in the Goddess becoming corporeal in us. For one year we became as faeries and were and lived as small, sparkling, winged nature spirits, full of joy, and some innocent mischief too. While I say nature spirit — because we could change our form to the invisible — we were of a natural body also.

This life ended one day, on what impulse I cannot describe. I can only say that an inner voice, the voice of the Goddess now a part of me, told me that it was time to resume our lives in the world. She would remain with me. We would be one, still me, not different than I was before, nor the same. Because the Goddess had given the faerie life to my companion also, we were in complete harmony.

We returned to the meadow and slept once again in the open in our faerie form. When we awoke, we were our human forms again, and only a single day and night had passed in the earthly world.

I said that you should consider this tale to be the narrative of a dream only — and in truth, on awakening again in the meadow, this very thing was my belief of it.

But my companion had the same full and detailed memory of our life together that past year in our other spirit form, which we discovered as we talked, and he expressed the belief that we had in truth experienced a genuine magical transformation.

It is not important to me whether you know this tale to be truth, but I would value your accepting my assurance that I completed the painting I have described, not in my imagination, but with real sticky tempera on hard board. Being of wit and intelligence, you will already have understood that each of the flowers I've described is also a faerie of our old acquaintance.

The last flower I have not told you, the most important.

This was bluebell, which carpeted our wood at the first moon of summer and dominated our hearts and thinking. Ours was and is a bluebell wood.

When I finished my painting and first showed him my work, my companion spoke to me in poetic language, in our Cornish, wherein he had woven words of his own for me with an old song of the Gaels about the forest trees.

It would render approximately thus.

As you were in the faerie mist,
so you will be again, my love.
Often will I call your name
and you will hear me,
remembering in its sound
who we are, sweet Angeline.

Already memory moves to vision
as images open behind my eyes,
confused, till we again gain power,
unclear, as the waters of a muddy
stream settle to clarify,
but which grow like the
trees of our ancient wood.

Oak, that warmed you
Pine, that smelled sweet
Birch, that burned too fast
Chestnut, so abundant
Hawthorn, which we cut in the fall
Holly, that burned like wax
Elm, smouldering without flame

Beech, which we kept for winter
Yew, that grew so slowly
Green Elder wood, a crime to sell
Pear and Apple, to scent your room
Ash-logs, aged smooth and grey
And Rowan, Alder, and Willow
Hazel, Cherry, Poplar, and Furze.

Priestess, your caring fills me
Priestess, your touch informs
Priestess, there is none so sensuous,
none thereby so capable to ever
renew the bond between us, fresh,
warming you, like Oak
smelling sweet, like Pine
quick burning, like Birch
abundant as Chestnut
slow growing, like Yew,
bring it to scent your heart
like the Pear and Apple branches
you kept fresh by your bedside.

Remembering the Future

2024

I

"It's not a spacecraft, and I've not come from another planet."

Vanessa remembered a *Far Side* cartoon she'd seen once. Not about space aliens or rocket ships, but about cats and dogs.

What we say. What they hear.

"I understand why you're afraid," Lillian added, trying to put her at ease. "What's your name?"

Vanessa struggled, but she couldn't make out what the woman was saying. Her brain just wouldn't free the resources.

Hearing what dogs hear, she thought, trying to repeat the sounds of the words in her mind.

The small wooden entry door hung open behind her, the strong sunlight beyond casting her in dark cameo for Lillian inside. She glanced to her left. The large sliding doors were closed tight.

They'd been wide open a few minutes before, and she'd seen the sleek silver vessel taxi inside. She could scarcely believe her eyes. There's lots of sightings in the New Mexico desert. No discoveries.

When she opened the small entry door and stepped inside, she was stunned to discover Lillian, right there in front of her. Naked from the waist up, with visibly strong arms, shapely tattooed breasts, and slim waist, wearing khaki combat pants and heavy black boots. Large handguns in thick leather holsters hung from both of her hips, carried on a broad fabric belt.

Alarmed, Vanessa's mind had clunked into stasis. She'd heard it stall. The same noise her boyfriend's pick-up truck made when its big-end bearings seized, trying to right the diesel pump on her uncle's farm after the tornado two years back.

Lillian was also startled on the instant but recovered as quickly. She liked her visitor. Liked the look of her. Athletic, even sensuous. She strained for a second to see if her breasts were ample, then felt silly and let a smile go to her lips. She hoped they might be friends.

"Come in, out of the sun. It's okay."

Lillian could clearly see the dog-brain effect in Vanessa's glazed expression.

Before Vanessa could recover, Lillian suddenly had an eye sensor sparkle.

Oh, blast. Into crisis.

Her powerful cyborg legs launched her forward, tackling her guest and dropping them both to the smooth gravel, Lillian taking Vanessa's weight on her back.

Releasing her, Lillian noticed the skin of her guest's slim waist was drawn over strong stomach muscles. A pretty face as well, with rough reddish hair tied back under a colourful cotton scarf.

Later, she thought.

"You were followed," Lillian whispered briskly in Vanessa's ear, pulling the woman to safety behind the rock edge, away from the wooden wall and doors. "Stay here."

Fist-sized holes were shattering open in the wall, the noise of each hit thundering through their chests, raising clouds of white smoke as they struck.

They're too high in the air, Lillian said to herself, reading the angles through the haze. Her vehicle and effects farther back in the cave were, as yet, undamaged.

They'll be coming back around, positioning for better trajectory, she thought as she scrambled up the steel ladder she'd installed through a narrow hole in the stone ceiling of the cave, to the gun turret she'd positioned above.

Quickly pulling herself into the gunner's chair, she secured her feet on the control pedals and attached the gunsight interface to her enhanced eye. Two launch barrels projected through the smooth half-sphere of transparent armour above. She pulled back the breech to load her artillery.

A glimpse of her attackers' faces was revealed in the gunsight as they flew by, well lit through their cockpit window in the sunshine.

Lillian locked on her target and pulled the trigger. The plasma rockets screamed as they flew. Two hits. The silver saucer dissolved into free molecules as it raced through the air overhead.

So where's that defense of killing in wartime when I need it? I'm sure I heard there was one! she thought. *Oh, bother. First sizing up the girl at the door so off-hand — then wasting these guys, even the genetic flotsam they were. What a mess a day can become.*

She straightened up and lay back in the chair.

Oh, well. These days are where I live. This brain is where I'm parked.

Coming back down the ladder into the cave, Lillian could see through the settling dust that her handsome wooden wall was pulverized, but no other damage was apparent.

"These guys weren't very good at this, really," she said quietly to Vanessa, walking over to the corner where she'd left her. Or Lillian thought she was speaking to her, but realized she was gone.

She scanned the back of the cave to see if the woman had escaped farther in or had run out. She had run out.

Lillian's legs couldn't move her at any exceptional speed, but they were quicker than flesh-and-blood legs and they didn't tire. Vanessa's fleeing footprints were obvious on the path down from the cave opening and Lillian soon caught up to her.

Vanessa didn't want to stop, nor did she want to speak, distress still in her eyes. But her chest was heaving with shortness of breath, and her legs were refusing to go any farther.

Lillian took her firmly by one arm, both to restrain her and help support her weight. In a comforting voice she said, "Relax yourself."

"I was so afraid," Vanessa answered, teary-eyed.

I don't think you'd have noticed if your hair was on fire, Lillian said to herself sympathetically.

She gave Vanessa a gentle embrace with one arm, which her new friend returned.

"It's okay now," Lillian said softly. "It's okay."

Lillian held Vanessa until her body relaxed. The skin of Lillian's exposed back and shoulders sweated in the desert sun, each drop evaporating as it emerged.

"Your stomach is all metal parts," her new friend said coyly.

"The legs too," Lillian calmly replied. "But I'm all natural from the diaphragm up and have all my organs, some nested down in the mechanicals."

Vanessa didn't know what to say. She looked blankly at Lillian, each with one arm still about the other.

"Um, almost all my organs. No kidneys. Synthetic filtration instead. Almost everyone has that. The metal parts give protection too, as long as I don't have a chubby tummy for padding!"

She smiled sweetly, realizing she had answered naïvely, as she would have spoken to someone at home.

"I'll explain later."

Lillian saw a hint of wounding in Vanessa's face.

"I will, I promise. But right now, let's get back to the cave, out of this blazing sun," she said. "It's torturous here in the open."

"Okay," Vanessa said.

Lillian took her hand, and they started back.

"I'm Vanessa."

"I'm Lillian."

"Um . . . big guns," Vanessa said blithely as they walked along.

"They're not heavy, just a little bulky."

"Did you use them to shoot down the UFO?" Vanessa asked.

"No, I have a more powerful cannon on the roof — though I prefer these. I'm nervous about explosives."

"Why did they attack us? Weren't they your people?"

"Not exactly," Lillian answered. "Truth is, I'm not completely sure, though I have a pretty good idea."

This wasn't the most urgent topic in Vanessa's mind.

"Are you really half mechanical?!" she asked. "I'm having some trouble grasping this!"

"I understand. Let me explain when we're out of the sun."

"Okay, Lillian."

They walked in silence, holding each others' hands. The grade was steep in places, and, taking her by the arm, Lillian tried to help Vanessa along.

They both watched the sky, even without wanting to, looking for vessels. Vanessa stumbled on a yucca plant as they did, and they both laughed.

"Guess I'd better watch where I'm going!" she said.

"No worries. There might easily be more. There will be more, sooner or later, I think. But if there were others in this group, we probably would've seen them by now."

Vanessa nodded.

"I have another similar shelter in Nevada. We'll go there."

"*We* will?" Vanessa shot back.

They were on the clearing in front of the hollow, just ahead of the shattered wall.

"Come inside, and we'll talk."

Vanessa stifled her anxiety and went in. She felt no threat from Lillian, even trusted and liked her. It had just been a lot to absorb in a short time.

Lillian led her inside, back to where she'd assembled a small living area — an oriental carpet on the smooth gravel floor, and on that a sofa, chair, dresser, bed, table, and lamps. Generators in her vehicle, parked adjacent, provided electric power.

She brought spring water to the cave in plastic cooler bottles, taken from supermarkets in nearby towns. She also took fresh fruits and other supplies.

She left cash after taking things. She just couldn't appear in person to pay.

"This is cozy!" Vanessa said.

"Thanks. I haven't had much time to enjoy it."

Lillian offered Vanessa a glass of cool water, which she accepted with a word of thanks and drank eagerly.

"There's a basin there if you want to wash your face."

"Okay, thanks, I will," Vanessa answered, then added, "Is that a Chinese coin you have tied to your belt?"

"No, it's a miniature of one of the stone coins from the South

Pacific. A good luck charm. There's a hole in the middle, but no writing like you'd find on a Chinese one."

Lillian pulled a short-sleeve shirt from a dresser drawer. Vanessa stared at the tattoos on her breasts as Lillian buttoned it up.

"What are those pictures?" she asked.

"This one," Lillian answered, pulling her shirt back open on the left side to show the tattoo, "is a wild boar, a symbol of the Great Goddess from the tenth century or so. This one," she continued, covering the left and opening the right, "represents the same, but with the moon."

"Wow! Amazing," Vanessa said. "But the tenth century where? On Earth, you mean?"

"Where else might I mean?" Lillian answered, confused.

"Um," is all Vanessa could find to say.

"Oh, you mean outer space or something!" Lillian continued with a smile, remembering she'd assured Vanessa against that same thing when she'd stood perplexed at the door earlier.

One thought fills immensity, she recalled from Blake.

"When you're chasing UFOs, you never expect to find one," Vanessa said. "The only one actually found, that we know about, was at Roswell, and that was carried off and hushed up. Of course, people are usually abducted by surprise, when they haven't been looking at all."

"Do I look like an alien?"

"No, not really," Vanessa said. "Except for the spaceship. And the robot parts. There's no robot parts like that for people on Earth."

"There isn't yet," Lillian said.

"What do you mean?"

"I mean I'm from Earth, like you. From Melbourne, Australia. The parts you see are made there and sold around the world."

"No they aren't! Those things don't exist!" Vanessa said stubbornly.

"Not yet they don't. But they will. You see, Vanessa, all of the UFOs you or anyone else have seen haven't been from outer space. They've come here from the future. From your own future, the future of this world."

2

"Can I go home to get some things?"

"Sure," Lillian answered. "You understand why you should come with me?"

"I don't mind coming. I enjoy the idea, actually. It's an adventure. A chance to see new things."

"I'm glad you have that attitude," Lillian said. "I'm only concerned for your safety, Vanessa. We're both tarred with the same brush now for those vandals; again, on the reasonable assumption there's others."

Lillian refilled Vanessa's water and sat beside her on the sofa, putting her holsters down on the carpet to one side. She leaned forward and unlaced her boots, pulling them off and rolling to one side to pile them beside the guns.

"*Callipygous!*" Vanessa said in a loud whisper.

"What?"

"Um, I enjoy unusual words — sorry," Vanessa answered quietly. "It's just for fun."

"No worries, I would enjoy that. But I don't know that one. 'Kallos' would be beauty, and 'pyge' . . ."

Vanessa grinned.

"Are you saying I have a nice ass?!"

They both laughed.

"Very glad you think so. Though it's factory sculpted, of course, so I can't take credit for it!"

Leaning her head back onto the sofa, Lillian pulled her feet up.

"This might not be the best time for us to rest, but it's less prudent to move while the sun's still up. Only three hours 'til sunset."

Vanessa finished her water and put down the glass, drawing up her legs and snuggling more closely into Lillian's body. Lillian raised an arm, guiding Vanessa's head to rest on her shoulder.

Vanessa was bursting with questions but was too tired to pursue them. She dozed off, and Lillian let her sleep. While she slept, Lillian poised her own mind to relax, caressing Vanessa's back and thigh as she lay in her arms.

I wonder if you know that I've been watching for you? Lillian said silently. *I wonder if you know how long?*

After an hour, she gave Vanessa a little shake to rouse her.

"Have I been sleeping?"

"About an hour," Lillian answered.

"Guess I needed that," she said with a smile. "I had such a dream! Do you have a pen? Something I'd like to note before I forget."

Lillian handed Vanessa a pen, and she wrote "Big Nose" in small letters on the side of her hand.

"It's a name, I think. A nickname that I heard in my dream."

Lillian just smiled and didn't pursue it.

"Would you like some coffee?"

"Do you have tea? I'd prefer tea. Just plain orange pekoe, please," Vanessa replied, adding a wince in case it was any bother.

"No worries," Lillian said. "Happen to have the very thing."

"Are we going soon?"

"It's still two hours before dark. About the time we'll need to pack up. We'll have to clear some of the debris at the door to get the vessel out as well."

"Can we stop at my house?"

"Don't worry," Lillian said smiling at her friend's apprehension.

"Sorry."

"Never mind. Isn't there anyone who'll miss you?"

"Yes, but not for a while. I came to New Mexico with my boy-friend three months ago. We'd been living in Houston, but he fell at work and cracked his head. We came out here to stay with his parents while he recovered. A few days ago, they sent him back to a hospital in Texas. So his parents think I'm back there, and my friends there think I'm here."

"Why didn't you go back?"

"Because I like it here, mainly. But also I'm interested in UFOs, and I saw you flying around a couple of days ago. That piqued my interest to stay longer. So I rented a guest room."

"Then this morning you saw me again."

"Yes. I only happened to be close to your cave here when you returned . . ."

Vanessa paused.

"From grocery shopping," Lillian said smiling, taking the cue.

"I was terrified opening the door, then even more so seeing you half-naked inside, looking mostly human. I expected a skinny body and big oval eyes in a great fat head, if anything. Funny how seeing a human form was more confusing!"

"That's what the guys I shot down looked like, more or less — the enlarged heads and eyes. Though not as bulbous as you'd see in your pop media."

"Why do they look like that, and you so normal? Apart from the metal bits."

"About them, I'm not completely clear, Vanessa. You might think I should know everything, but I don't."

Vanessa assured Lillian she had no such expectation, putting her arm around Lillian's shoulders and squeezing her warmly, her other hand resting motionless on Lillian's breast.

"I do know they're from the future. Not only your future, but my future also. Some time in the distant future. They may look more advanced because of their science-fiction physiques, but they're not. The big head is a degraded form, I think, gradually corrupted over thousands of years."

"But their spaceship looked just like yours," Vanessa said.

"Yes, it was mine. Someone in that distant future must've found my equipment," Lillian said, and laughed. "But they found no weaponry, and what they did manage to put together in that respect is somewhat primitive, I think."

"Yes," Vanessa said.

"But I don't know why they came here, or why they'd want to destroy me."

"You don't?"

"No. My coming to this time had nothing to do with them. I was completely surprised when I realized there were others from my own time here."

"Why did you come?"

"Because I discovered the means, I suppose. Simple as that."

"You discovered how to move in time without intending to?"

"Not exactly. I was interested in space travel — looking for a way to cross the vastness of galactic space over the folds in time. Like you might skip a rock over water."

"Maybe you could still do that."

"Possibly. But I haven't figured it out. How to reposition an object in space across those fold tops, I mean. Moving to a different space in the same time. There are critical ambiguities. But I accidentally worked out how to reposition myself to another time in the same space. That was a different quantity."

"Don't people speak differently in the future? In your time, I mean? You sound just like me!" Vanessa said brightly.

"There's fewer people as a whole later — nature rebelled against humankind with terrible plagues when it became overwhelmingly successful. More successful than now, in this time I mean, in sheer numbers. A vast sea of humanity, if you'll forgive the cliché."

"So, technology couldn't come to the rescue finally," Vanessa popped in.

"Something like that. It started with the Industrial Revolution. Trouble was, the new machinery created a significant surplus. But everyone's DNA was still working on the old programming — to reproduce as aggressively as possible. Which excess the new industrial surplus fed."

"Even before oil and gas."

"Steam engines were coal driven, so more than a few dead dinosaurs went to the furnace even then. But it all escalated greatly with cheap fuel oil."

"It's still escalating now."

Lillian nodded.

"Without which growth," Vanessa added, "a smaller population could've enjoyed the surplus much longer. But it swelled instead."

"Yes. But not far ahead a big wind-down is coming."

"Fills me with dread," Vanessa said. "And so easy to predict."

"You have a word for it?" Lillian added with a little smile, trying to lighten the mood.

"Um, *peripateia* maybe. A sudden change of fortune."

"A lot of people plunged into the Bardo at once, anyway."

"I wonder if they had enough beds?" Vanessa said lightly.

Lillian smiled.

"It's so strange talking to someone who knows the future! I can't get over it. So very strange!" Vanessa continued.

"When I first realized I'd have the means, it wasn't knowing how this or that might emerge in the future that had appeal for me. It was going back and repairing mistakes in the past."

"What mistakes do you mean?"

"My own mistakes."

"Oh! And did you?"

"Coming here was my first experiment. So, no, I haven't yet. Truth is, I realized I couldn't. At least, travelling back to your own past you're not reliving your life again. The older you from the future is just there in the same time and space as the younger you, both doing exactly what they did originally. I mean, whatever the older you might try to do, things would only be affected to their original course and outcome."

"Yes, but it seems strange that an older you and a younger you might come face-to-face in the same time!"

"I think I'll avoid putting that to the test," Lillian said.

"I'm sorry you have these mistakes you want to fix."

Lillian drew a fingertip through the condensation on the side of her water glass.

Objects in the rear-view mirror may appear closer than they are, she mused.

"Way back to your question, the languages people speak in my time are much the same as you have now," Lillian continued, "just evolved further. English and Chinese are dominant. Your English sounds to me like Shakespearean English sounds to you."

"But you sound exactly the same as me!" Vanessa said again, with slight exasperation.

"Yes, given you speak like a well-educated person, without a lot of ornaments or slang. I have a sensor in my middle parts that picks up wave energy from your speech centre and sends a signal to mine. So I can mimic you, if you like, for better communication."

"Kind of a universal translator?"

"No — or maybe it is. I was going to say dumbing down my English to yours wasn't a translation, but I guess it is."

"That sensor seems so remarkable, I'm skeptical it could exist. But then I'm amazed with a lot of the technologies we have here in my time, and don't understand how most of them work."

"It doesn't power my brain to speak any language I want, or add words to my vocabulary. You can get translation tools like that, so you can understand other languages, and many people do, but I wanted to keep the overhead down with mine. I have translation tools available in the vehicle if I need them."

"Speaking of which, I guess we had better get up and get that thing packed," Vanessa said deliberately.

"Yes. I have only what you see here, and the gun turret, all of which will fit in the hold."

Lillian eased Vanessa off her and pulled on her boots and belt.

"I have a high-tech handcart to help with the heavy lifting. Why don't you start by sealing the dresser drawers. If you can get the furniture off the carpet, you could roll that up. I'll take the cart and bring the turret down."

"Okay," Vanessa said.

Lillian went up around the side of the outcrop in the dusk light to remove the turret. She kept low, scanning the sky as she went. After removing its moorings, the turret lifted out in one large roughly-spherical piece, which Lillian, lying on her back, pushed into the cart jaws with her mechanical legs.

While she was making the turret fast to the cart, an eye sensor sparkled. She spotted the enemy off in the distant sky.

Another vehicle of her design, she observed. No doubt about it.

They hadn't had the wit or means to improvise any change, as far as I can tell, she thought.

It was moving away to the northwest.

They don't seem to have noticed me.

She wondered how there could be three vehicles. She'd built only one. Thus far, at least.

Why, if I'm having this trouble now, would I build more machines later?

Possibilities began looping in her mind.

SOME SUNNY DAY : 2024

"Moving in time certainly confounds our comfortably linear perception of things," she muttered out loud.

But I'm aging, just the same. And will die.

The second vessel hadn't resumed the attack, but she still affirmed her decision to move to the other homesite in the Nevada desert.

She gazed up at the sky. Stars were beginning to emerge in the fresh darkness.

I will die, sooner or later, just the same, she repeated to herself. *Skipping over the centuries can give the illusion of escaping that. But no one does. You wouldn't want to be around forever anyway, long-suffering in this suffering world. You want just long enough to conquer it. Like Milarepa, or Padmasambhava.*

Coming into the cave with the turret, Lillian could see Vanessa had applied herself with considerable effort. The furnishings and effects were neatly piled beside her vehicle, the area swept clean.

"I can't wait to see what it's like inside!" Vanessa said with real pleasure in her voice.

"Somewhat spartan, I'm afraid," Lillian said with a wink. "You want to do the honours?"

"Sure!" Vanessa said.

"It works with an entry keyword, tied to an iris scan. I can do a code for you now."

Vanessa was looking at Lillian as she listened, unaware she was being screened for an iris pattern.

"Now look at the panel, and punch 1, 7, 8 on the keypad."

Vanessa did so, and the door opened to one side. A ramp folded down for their entry.

"You built this?" Vanessa asked in fresh amazement.

"Yes, I did. All by myself. It took about three years to complete, working full time."

"How could you afford to do that? Don't people have to earn a living in the future?"

"Yes, but people — then and now — can accumulate enough for a sabbatical. I only worked as long as I needed to keep body and soul together. I got a break on my mature-body parts, offering services in contra to other engineers. Most governments have socialized essential parts for children now. 'Now' meaning my 'now.' When I left to come here."

"Easy to get confused," Vanessa said with a smile.

"Yes!" Lillian replied.

Lillian opened the door to the hold, inside to the right of the entry, and they carried in the furniture and supplies.

"What were you like when you were born?" Vanessa asked.

"I was a baby."

Vanessa laughed, as though this was only a joke — a humorous reply to an obvious question — then realized it might not be obvious at all.

"Are some people in the future not babies when they're born?"

"No, they're all babies. I was kidding. Some used to be grown in artificial wombs, but that's frowned upon now."

"Interesting. Why is that?"

"Because you don't have a spirit if you're not born naturally, from a woman. No ancient soul will claim the body. Artificials weren't evil, they were just empty, even to themselves. No one wanted the ethical burden of raising humanoid slaves, so the technology was abandoned. There's robots for the mundane work."

"But you're part machine. Were you born missing some pieces?"

"Yes, I was. Birth defects like that are common. We don't like to admit it, but we're already into decline genetically in my time. Homo sapiens, I mean. Improvements or repairs made at different stages only made it worse in the long run. Populations are much reduced from what you have now, as I told you before."

"So the bug-eyed guys are the progression of that, another few hundred years down the road?"

"Another few thousand, I think — but, yes, that's the idea."

"Huh," Vanessa replied.

They carried the sofa aboard, then Lillian used the cart to carry the dresser in, and they closed the hold.

"We'll get your things and add them in. Do you think there's enough room left?"

"Plenty," Vanessa answered. "I just have a few clothes, and some jewelry and toiletries."

"This is the sleeping deck," Lillian said, raising a panel behind the cockpit.

The cabin was little larger than the inside of a commercial van, finished in smooth grey alloy. Lillian's welds and assembly were neat as a pin, but it was still apparent the vessel was home built.

"It's only one cot but should be large enough for us, when we stay in here."

"That'll be nice," Vanessa said, a little sparkle coming into her eyes.

"There's a co-pilot seat, so you can sit up in the forward section with me."

Vanessa was glancing around, looking for anything else still undiscovered.

"That's about all we got," Lillian said, seeing Vanessa's gestures. "Most of the bulk of the vehicle is made up of coils that charge the local fabric — the material fabric of space — so we can slip peak-to-peak in time. They also make us effectively weightless . . ."

"So we can fly through the air!" Vanessa said.

"That's right," Lillian said smiling. "There's a reactor for operating power. The fuel lasts for months, so no worries about finding a petrol station. Oh, and the toilet is here," she added, raising an entry panel to one side of the sleeping cabin. "We haven't lost those bio-parts or processes. Speaking of which, as soon as we get going we can have something to eat."

"I always thought it was odd there were no toilets on *Star Trek*. Nobody asking permission to scoot off the bridge for a pit stop."

"In the science-fiction movie? The same in most films, I think, unless they're making a point of that realism."

They moved into the cockpit, taking their respective seats. Lillian reached over to show Vanessa how to secure her flight belts.

"Although weightless, more or less, there's lurches and groans from time to time as we move along," Lillian said. "And some little wows in your brain when we're moving through the matrix."

"You can control this slipping across time folds? I mean, you can pick a particular time to go to?" Vanessa asked, snapping her last buckle into place.

"I can once I've been there but can only make a guess — hopefully a good guess — going somewhere for the first time. Each moment in the field has a kind of sound signature, which I can record and replicate once I've been there. But if we wanted to go and see the dinosaurs I'd have to estimate and just give it a shot."

"Well, with a 450-million-year window there, I'm sure you'd manage to zoom in somewhere in range."

Vanessa was just trying to say something positive, but Lillian smirked.

"Yes, shouldn't be hard to throw a pebble into that bucket," she said, and they laughed.

"But we can't go to our attackers' time exactly until we've been there. One of those little ambiguities. Can't possibly guess."

"Unless we were to know the signature in advance, from the records on their ship for instance," Vanessa said.

"That's right!" Lillian said. "You're hot!"

"Not hot enough to know how we might accomplish that."

"Quite," Lillian said. "But we need that opportunity, however it happens."

"Who's this on the dashboard?" Vanessa asked, gesturing to a small bronze figure beside a window strut in front of her.

"That's Tara," Lillian explained, "White Tara — a Tibetan Goddess. She has seven eyes, which symbolize the watchfulness of the compassionate mind. There's also Green Tara, who's similar but doesn't have the additional eyes and sits in a different posture. They say Tara brings long life to her devotees, and always comes swiftly when she's called for aid."

"That's interesting. I thought I knew a little about Buddhism, but I don't know this one."

"There's quite a few to know, I guess, for the Tibetan guys especially," Lillian replied. "In history, White Tara and Green Tara were incarnated as Tritseun and Wen-ch'eng, respectively the Nepalese and the Chinese wives of the Tibetan King Songtsen Gampo, who died about 650 A.D."

"You know a lot!"

"Never mind, there's much more than that."

"Why would a Buddhist be worried about long life, when that philosophy is about clearing the deck?" Vanessa asked.

"There are different schools of Buddhism, of course. But in general, life is your only opportunity to develop. Though I don't think Buddhist practice is about 'clearing the deck.' That's just the outcome of complete mindfulness."

"How's that?"

"Your identity, your knowledge of yourself, comes from memory, whether memories of your life now, or those earlier, if you're gifted to remember your distant past. These memories not only tell you *who* you are but also *that* you are."

"That's interesting," Vanessa said. "You should've been a college professor, Lillian."

"I know I sound like one sometimes. Sorry about that."

"Never mind. Though I don't make the connexion here yet!"

"Well, your memory is always a split second behind the present moment. If your mindfulness practice moves your whole being into that pure present instant, both who you are and that you are are gently disconnected."

"*Who* you are and *that* you are," Vanessa said thoughtfully.

"Brings a word to mind?"

"Um," Vanessa said. "*Hendiadys* perhaps."

"Good one!" Lillian said.

"Allowing a little slack," Vanessa replied with a smile.

Lillian was pressing square buttons on the flight panel ahead of her, which lit up the cabin with glows of peach, rose, and lilac.

"It's a frightening thought, really — about going there. The distant future seems dangerous and ugly," Vanessa said.

3

"What beautiful horses!"

Vanessa was out in the sunshine in front of the Nevada retreat.

"They're wild. Probably not many wild horses left in America, but there are some," Lillian said. "Mostly latter generations of escapes from the Spanish explorers."

"These don't seem wild — apart from showing up here. They're so friendly toward you, Lillian. Even warm."

"Horses are highly telepathic."

"And no doubt you have an enhancer in your bag of wires for that," Vanessa replied.

Lillian laughed and squeezed her hand.

"Yes, actually, I do."

"Can you hear what the horses think?"

"I can somewhat," Lillian said, "and they can hear and understand what I say."

"They seem to trust you."

The horses, a mare and its two-year-old filly, were returning after cantering away down the valley. When they reached the clearing where the women stood, they came over and dropped a gathering of grasses at their feet.

"They've brought us food," Lillian said.

"Wow! That's so nice!" Vanessa said, keeping her distance from the horses.

"Thank you," Lillian said to the mare. "Thank you."

The horse came to Lillian and nuzzled the nape of her neck with its nose. The filly remained behind.

Stroking the mare's head, Lillian said, "Your daughter is shy, handsome mother."

How we speak to horses, Vanessa thought to herself.

"So is my friend," Lillian continued. "Or rather, she doesn't know how to show you she's friendly."

The mare raised its head and, with a shake side-to-side, let out a whinny. To Vanessa's surprise, the filly came to her and pushed her shoulder with its head. Vanessa recoiled slightly but marshalled herself and reached out and stroked the horse's nose.

"We have work to do," Lillian said to the mare. "We need to make this place safe."

The horse gave a loud snort from its nostrils and lowered its shoulder, bending its right front knee.

"She's offering to help us," Lillian said to Vanessa.

"We can use your great strength, thank you," Lillian said to the mare, then added whimsically, "But your beauty and freedom we can only admire."

The horse shook its head.

"She approves of you, I think," Vanessa said.

"We are under threat here, from evil people," Lillian explained to the horse. "We need to move some big stones down to disguise and protect our shelter."

The mare snorted again, then turned and loped back down the valley with its filly.

"What does that mean?!" Vanessa asked.

"I'm not sure!" Lillian said, "but I know they mean to help."

"Getting more grass to keep us fed, I guess."

"That would be a way of helping for them," Lillian said.

"Oh, yes!" Vanessa answered. "I know that!"

The arrangement of the Nevada hideout was different from the place in New Mexico. Instead of one large cave, there were two smaller ones at different elevations, connected by a shaft inside the hill, the remnants of an abandoned silver mine.

The vehicle was parked in the lower, a large cave cut deep into the rock face at the level of the broad valley. Stowed well back, it was safely out of sight and could be flown straight out, with no need for hangar doors. Lillian renovated a mineshaft ladder so she could get back and forth to the vehicle without going outside.

The upper level, below the flat top of the silver hill about fifty feet above, was also a cave, dug out of the rock face by the miners.

There was an old wooden facing structure already there when Lillian found the spot, which she renovated inside. The outside she left untouched, preserving its abandoned appearance.

But now she wanted to cover the facing with stone for protection. There was plenty of rubble on the hilltop above. They just had to move it over the edge of the ridge, down in front of the wall.

Lillian brought Vanessa inside to get some ropes for the job.

"It's so cool in here!" Vanessa said.

"Yes, a kind of natural air conditioning. Cold air is drawn up the mineshafts, hundreds or thousands of feet below ground."

"Amazing!"

"Do you mind if I have my shirt off for this?" Lillian asked.

"No, not at all — though I don't know how you can tolerate the chafing of ropes against your skin."

They both lifted coils of rope on either shoulder and carried them outside. The ropes were old, left there by the miners, but still strong. There were various leftovers lying about throughout the mine.

They'd arrived in the dark just before dawn, first bringing the vehicle down on the upper-level clearing to unload their furnishings and supplies, then flying it around to park in the hangar at ground level. They reassembled Lillian's living room on the oriental carpet, rolled out in the middle of the cave floor, which had been groomed smooth by its original tenants long before.

"We'll make a big rope basket, to pull the rock down from above."

Stepping out into the morning sun, they worked together uncoiling the ropes. They went back inside for some shorter lengths, which they tied into a basketweave between the longer to drag rock from the hilltop down in front of the old wooden facing.

"This is great having all of this fat rope handy, but how are we going to move the rock? I can barely lift the rope all tied together like this, much less filled with rock!" Vanessa said.

"We'll have to get the Silver Surfer for that," Lillian answered, referring to her vehicle. "We'll pull our hoop up around the rubble above and attach the ends to the craft. Though I hate to bring it out again in daylight."

"Oh! You won't have to!" Vanessa said. "Look!"

She pointed up behind them to the hilltop above the wooden wall.

"Wow!" Lillian exclaimed.

Looking down on them were eleven large wild horses, including her friend the mare. When Lillian looked up, they began nodding their heads and flaring their nostrils, some stamping their front hooves on the ground.

4

"So you came back in time to see if your machine would work?"

"More or less. I wasn't looking for anything," Lillian replied.

"No urge to haul back spices and teakwood or anything like that. It was scientific interest. Wasn't going to build it without trying it out, naturally."

Evening had progressed, and they were lying together in bed. Vanessa wore a nightshirt, Lillian was in her briefs.

"I thought you might be looking for a better place to live. Cleaner air, better food, that sort of thing."

"I couldn't do that really. There's no one back in time who can fix my body parts when they need repair."

"Oh!" Vanessa exclaimed, "I didn't think of that."

She gazed at Lillian tenderly and with sympathy. She brought herself forward and kissed her gently on the lips.

"You could always stay here, and just go back when you need something," Vanessa said expectantly. "Unless you really miss Australia, that is. Australia in your time."

"I've been thinking about that," Lillian said with a little wink, "though I do love Australia. The aboriginals especially have a naturally mystic nature, which I feel a strong bond with. My good friend Roderick is an aborigine."

"Is he your boyfriend?"

"No, he has another girlfriend. We're all close though. We're on faculty together at the same research institute."

"I have a boyfriend, but he's a dunce. We just argue all the time, about trivial things."

"Are you often with women?" Lillian asked quietly.

"No, I haven't been before," Vanessa answered. "But you're different. Very different."

"I used to worry if I was going to fry in hell for it," Lillian said and laughed.

"You worry about religious things?"

"Absolutely. I'm not usually so vocal as I am with you — and I tend to lecture, as you know already! — but I'm religious above all. Just took me a while to settle on my chosen deity. As you can see by the tattoos, that was the Goddess of the Celts, the White Goddess, for quite a long time. That had a natural evolution, some process of its own, to Tara."

"You've kept the tattoos, though."

"They're still the common inflexion in my heart. Not the same, and not different."

"Do you think the White Goddess — the one in your tattoos — would have known about the decline of humankind, or even its extinction, a few thousand years ahead? And might have instructed some of her devotees with that awareness?"

"Certainly she would have."

Vanessa snuggled in closer to Lillian's side, resting her face on the side of one breast.

"I'm so sorry you can't feel me touch you below the middle."

"But I can, Vanessa. I have relays all over the surface where it's artificial," she said. Moving Lillian's hand up her inner thigh, she continued, "and still have my own tissues in here."

Vanessa smiled.

"I'm sorry those guys came here from the future. If they hadn't, no one'd know you're here, and you wouldn't have anything in particular you needed to do, right?"

"That's right. Nobody but you, anyway."

"Nobody but me what?" Vanessa asked.

"Nobody but you would know I was here."

"There were probably others who saw the ship," Vanessa said. "But people see UFOs all the time, and no one believes much of it. Anyway, it's usually an hallucination, the way people used to see great armies of warriors up in the clouds in the middle ages."

Lillian curled herself over away from Vanessa, reaching for their mugs of water.

"Mustn't forget to keep drinking water."

"An extra three or four quarts a day in the desert, I know."

They both drank.

"Oh, that's good," Lillian said.

Vanessa playfully sprinkled the last of hers down the middle of Lillian's chest. Lillian laughed and spun around, wrestling Vanessa onto her back and leaning over her, pinning her wrists to the bed on either side with her hands.

"Oh, yeah?" Lillian said grinning.

"Yeah!" Vanessa answered in mock defiance.

Lillian pursed her cheeks and delivered a quick thin stream of water from between her teeth to the shallow of Vanessa's neck.

Laughing, Vanessa struggled out from under her.

"Do you have art and music and stuff like that where you come from?" she asked as they eased and lay together again.

"Sure we do!" Lillian replied. "It's one thread of history. Only this era is a part of mine, the way ancient Rome is a part of yours."

"So they might have my nightie in a museum?"

"Absolutely. And your toothbrush, hair dryer, and dental floss. Not to mention personal computers, smudge pots, silverware, coffee cups, motorcycles, and comic books."

"Guess you could clean up in the antique market, being able to come back and buy the stuff new at Wal-Mart."

"Yes, I suppose I could. Hadn't thought of that!" Lillian said.

"We'd be rich!" Vanessa said.

"Oh *we* would, would we? Partners then?"

"Absolutely! But doesn't anyone in your time know you've gone?"

"Only two close friends."

"If they let this out, the trade in antiquities could collapse!"

"They're sworn to secrecy — but not on account of profiteering. There's political consequences, too dangerous to ever cross. Knowledge of this will die with the three of us."

"Well, it may do, but someone has discovered how it works."

"Yes, indeed — they have the tools anyway. I doubt they know how it works. The vehicles we saw are my workmanship, not just made from my plans. It would be difficult to work out the method by examining the finished components."

"I don't understand. Why would you make more of them, when you know now they'll be stolen by these nefarious characters?"

"I asked myself the same thing, but obviously I did. Or will, that is. There's a paradox in the middle, of course — that if I went forward into my time and, having this knowledge, didn't make them, then there'd be nothing for them to steal in the future, and the attack yesterday afternoon wouldn't have happened. So I'd go ahead and make them later."

"Say again?"

"If I choose not to make the vehicles because I've learned they'll be stolen later, then nothing would happen here, and I'd get back home and freely choose to make them. In which case, the attack would happen here. After which, you wouldn't think I'd choose to make them."

"I get it."

"It's hard to express! A paradox looping on a condition."

"There's *epexegesis* about most of this," Vanessa said with a smile and a wink.

"Explanations of explanations, indeed."

"Including about how they know you are here. Finding your equipment didn't include any kind of locator for you, did it?" Vanessa asked.

"No, not that I know. Unless I leave it for them. I must have."

"We may never find out."

"I have the feeling we will," Lillian said. "I think we must."

Before she'd finished her sentence, Vanessa flung a cushion in Lillian's face, and then another, laughing and shouting "Pillow fight! Pillow fight!"

"Hey! Are you stooping to *gargalesis*?!" Lillian said laughing, as Vanessa put her hands to her ribs. "See, I know a few words too!"

5

"Now we're settled here, I'd like to go back and stake out the old place."

"Oh?" Vanessa replied, hearing some doubt in Lillian's voice.

"Though I'm not sure how we'll otherwise pass the time there, if we do. It'll be like a duck hunter sitting in a blind all day."

"Seems an incredibly dull activity!" Vanessa said.

They were on the sofa in their livingroom space.

"Yes, brutally dull, but they still do it," Lillian said.

And they kill for amusement, she thought. *Figure that out if you can.*

"Others have patient work too," Vanessa added. "Like nature photographers, who often have terrific long waits before getting the shot they want. Can't just ask a bird or a bee to do this or that. Have to wait for it."

"I'd feel better if we knew our buddies were coming back."

"You'd think they'd still be looking for you. But would they think you'd stay there after the first attack?"

Lillian got up to her feet and stood facing Vanessa.

"Whatever they think, they'll come and look," Lillian said.

"They may already have," Vanessa replied.

"They'd probably check again, in case we were just lying low."

"If you want to bait them, why don't we make some repairs to the front doors and wall. That'll fool 'em."

"Yes, it will — good idea!" Lillian said with some enthusiasm, turning and dropping herself back on the sofa beside Vanessa.

"We'll leave in two hours, when it's dark."

"Sure," Vanessa said. Then, after a pause, she added, "Oh! look! We have a visitor. Two visitors."

Through the front door, now hidden behind a mound of rocks, they could see the two horses that had befriended them.

"I think they want us to come out and play."

"Yes, they want to take us for a ride," Lillian said.

"An unusual honour to ride on a wild horse," Vanessa said as they both ran lightly to the door.

"Are you sure you want to do this?" Lillian said to the mare when they were outside.

The horse nodded its head.

Neither were experienced saddle riders, much less bareback with no halter and reins, so both were awkward at first. Lillian managed to pull herself up and onto the horse, but Vanessa had some trouble and had to get the horse to come over beside a large rock, so she could gain some height.

They rode off, and it wasn't long before they both found their balance, their legs between the horses' barrel and shoulders, and their hands holding the base of their manes.

The horses kept mostly to an easy canter. While Lillian and Vanessa were talking and having fun, it gradually dawned on Lillian that for the horses this wasn't a recreational ride.

After a few miles, they came to a spring hidden in the mouth of a cave, where the horses stopped to drink.

The passage was low, and the women had to dismount for the horses to get in.

After they were refreshed and about to leave, Lillian asked the mare if they were taking them somewhere in particular. The horse nodded in the affirmative and shook its nose to the west.

"Okay," Lillian said, "let's see what it is."

"It'll be dark soon," Vanessa said once safely on the filly's back again. "If we're still thinking about the stake-out, that is."

"We'll have to play it by ear, I guess."

"Sure," Vanessa said.

Lillian saw they were approaching a town. The horses brought them into some thick brush beside an old gas station just off the highway and stopped.

Lillian and Vanessa got down. They could see the horses were making an effort to be as quiet as possible, and they followed suit.

They made their way toward the station, first crouching and then on their hands and knees.

As they approached the edge of the brush they could see it. One of Lillian's silver vehicles, parked behind the diesel pump to one side of the service building.

"They're inside," Lillian whispered. "I think they're asleep."

"They'd be living in the craft while they're away, of course" Vanessa whispered back.

"There's no one working here," Lillian said, turning her atten-tion to the gas station. "This is a keylock pump. The service centre is abandoned."

"Yes, I can see that. The sign over there says 'White Rose.' Never heard of that," Vanessa whispered.

"That marquee is probably seventy-five years old," Lillian replied. "See, the lit sign up beside the highway is for Mobil."

"Yes. So what do we do now?"

"We wait for a while."

Lillian turned to see if the horses were still there. They were sitting motionless, with their legs curled to one side beneath them.

"Thank you for this. But it looks like we'll be a while," Lillian said in a loud whisper, to which the horses nodded.

It wasn't long before a truck pulled off the highway into the key-lock. Lillian and Vanessa could see the faces of the alien pilots through the cockpit window, their heads laid back with their eyes closed.

"They're still working on that beauty sleep."

"Wow! They *really* need it too!" Vanessa whispered in reply. "Are they ever ugly!"

They saw the grey faces of the alien pilots awaken suddenly and gawk out into the darkness. They rose from their seats.

"They're coming out!" Lillian said. "Here's the plan."

Lillian pulled a handgun out of its holster with her left hand and primed it with her right.

"You're going to have to go in there, 'cause you don't know how to use one of these yet," holding up her big revolver. "I'll cover you. You'll only have a minute or two at best. You have to take their position beacon and origin time signatures — you remember how to do that?"

Vanessa nodded, thinking how fortunate it was Lillian had shown her these procedures, passing the time on the way to Nevada from New Mexico.

"And see what they've got in the hold, if you have time. I'll whistle when it's time to get out, if you haven't already. Just get out fast! Okay?"

The creatures stepped out onto the pavement. Their craft was on the opposite side of the keylock pump from where the semi-tractor driver was starting to fill his big fuel tanks. They came around in sight of the driver.

"Okay, go!" Lillian whispered.

Vanessa quietly sprinted for the ship, while Lillian positioned herself behind an empty propane tank along the back wall of the station, where she could see the creatures approaching the luckless truck driver, and also the timecraft. She couldn't see past the door of the vehicle, but she could see Vanessa up to the moment she went inside.

Lillian was tense.

She saw the driver sputtering with fear as he saw the brutes approach, shaking and losing possession of himself, and was filled with anger and remorse that she could not, or would not, come to the driver's aid. It was more important that Vanessa get those time signatures and see what their cargo was, if she could.

I could shoot them dead and spare this guy, but then we might never know what's going on. Which, if we don't find out, could mean many more lives.

Vanessa was back outside in less than two minutes.

Which was just in time, it turned out, because the creatures had already tied and gagged the truck driver and were leading him back to the craft.

No introductions or small talk goin' on there, Lillian thought.

When Vanessa was safely back, hiding in the brush with the horses, Lillian rushed through the darkness to join them.

Vanessa was visibly shaken.

"There are people in there," she whispered to Lillian. "Five people. All tied up, with their faces taped over. It was horrible to see. There were bloody needle marks, like they'd been given injections, clumsily. Their skin was cold, but I tried two of them for a pulse and they were still living."

"Captives for some terrible purpose."

"But for what?"

6

"Lillian, I'm so relieved you're safe! I can hardly believe my eyes!" Roderick said joyfully.

Lillian and Vanessa were at the door to Roderick's flat.

"Come in! Justine's here," he continued, then called "Justine!"

"This is my friend Vanessa," Lillian said to Roderick as they went into his living room, where Justine was sitting.

Justine got up and gave Lillian a hug.

"This is my friend Vanessa," Lillian repeated to Justine.

Justine took Vanessa's hands in hers and made her welcome.

"Can I get you anything?" Roderick asked.

"A beer would be good," Lillian said. "Will you have one, Vanessa?"

"Sure, thanks."

Lillian sat on the sofa next to Justine.

"I guess you've been to your place already," Justine said.

"Yes! What's the story?!" Lillian answered intently.

"Guess we're failures as house-sitters," Roderick said, handing them their drinks, then pulling up a chair for himself.

"Not at all," Lillian said, "but what happened?"

"The strangest intruders," Justine said. "We were going in to check up on things and caught them in the act."

"Coming out down the stairs, anyway," Roderick interjected.

"We tidied up as well as we could. It was a much bigger mess to begin with."

"I could see things were out of place," Lillian said. "Did you see the villains?"

"They looked like mutants," Roderick said. "They came in your time machine."

"What!" Justine burst in. "You didn't tell me that!"

"No, I'm sorry Justine."

"You're fired!"

" I didn't want to worry you before we knew if Lillian was okay or not. I'm sorry if that was the wrong thing to do."

"I think it was, but that's okay. Damned if you do and damned if you don't, I suppose, and you did the more considerate thing. But you should have said, regardless," Justine replied.

"It isn't my machine, which I have with me now. It's another that we'll make here, in our future. At least two more, actually, maybe three," Lillian said.

"You'll make two or three more of them, knowing they'll fall into the hands of criminals?" Justine asked, surprise in her face.

"That's what I said!" Vanessa added.

"I don't know the reason, but we'll make that choice. You saw we did — or rather, will — when you saw the other machine. It'll become clear as events unfold, I'm sure."

"Do you know what they took, if anything?" Roderick asked.

"Roddy and I couldn't tell if anything was gone. He thought they must've been after some specific information," Justine added.

"Yes, they were. I had the advantage of knowing just what I was looking for," Lillian said, "being biotech data. The CyBio method for rejuvenating corrupt cells in particular. It was first developed by a biologist named Johnson, a U.S. Peace Corps volunteer from Fiji, who later defected to the defense industry. Anyway, I needed to see for myself what I had along that line here at home."

"And was it accessed?" Justine asked.

"Yes."

"How on earth did you know to look for that?" Roderick said.

"I just had a hunch, bringing some Holmesian deduction to the evidence."

"You guys still have Sherlock Holmes?" Vanessa blurted out.

"Ever popular," Justine answered with a smile.

"But I've not solved the case," Lillian continued, "though I have this clue to go on. The truth is, I wasn't surprised to find I'd been burgled. Though I couldn't know what information they might've found, or in what time. Ours or theirs, I mean."

"Who are these guys?"

"Corrupt homo erectus," Vanessa said.

"I don't know the details," Lillian added, "but we have their time signature, which is a long way in the future."

"How far?" Justine asked.

"About fifty-seven hundred years."

"Huh. Clearly things don't improve for the gene pool," Roderick said dryly.

"How did you get involved in this, Vanessa?" Justine asked.

"I just happened onto the spot when Lillian arrived."

"They attacked my shelter moments later," Lillian said.

"She dissolved them," Vanessa said. "It was upsetting seeing it."

"I'm sure it was!" Justine said sympathetically.

"Another of your vessels?" Roderick asked.

"No doubt about it," Lillian said.

"Well, if you have the time signature, maybe a trip to their home destination would be clarifying."

"I guess that's next," Lillian said.

"They won't be happy with that CyBio procedure," Roderick said in a low voice.

"Why not?" Vanessa asked.

"It doesn't work," Roderick replied. "Even Marty Schwartz, our best man in medical, couldn't solve that one."

"The cost of their iniquity," Lillian said.

"Fifty-nine dollars," Vanessa muttered.

"What was that, Vanessa?" Roderick asked.

"Sorry, just something my mother used to say," she replied with a blush. "There was a motel down the road from us where I grew up. When we drove by, she would sometimes repeat the nightly rate they posted, saying this was the 'cost of iniquity.' Over my head as a child."

Justine laughed. "Things mothers say."

"I was referring to the innocent lives spent," Lillian said.

7

"This is like Christmas shopping."

Lillian laughed and asked, "Why is that?"

"Before I say, do you have Christmas shopping still?" Vanessa said.

"There's still Christmas, but scarce resources slowed the shopping frenzy well before my time."

They were belted in their seats in Lillian's vehicle, talking while they flew over a dense, humid jungle below.

"Our economy is based on consumption. We can't imagine any other kind," Vanessa said.

"Yes, I know. That changed, of necessity. But a shocking blowout while it lasted! Our historians look back on that era as reigned by a kind of mass insanity."

"We went through that black gold pretty quick anyway."

"Pretty quick! Wow! You sure did. Like one of those pub contests to see who can drink the most beer at one sitting. How was it possible to burn that much fuel in such a short time?"

"Guess it all ran out, right?"

"Injury made no one wiser, and it went down to the last drop. Alternates were available — solar, wind, and nuclear — but they weren't as economical."

"Nuclear isn't all that attractive, is it? Lots of waste that never breaks down."

"We shipped it into space."

"What?" Vanessa said, and laughed. "But so much weight!"

"Somebody came up with a kind of elevator. A long super-fiber cable attached to the ground that went straight up into space, however many miles that is. It was kept taut by the earth's motion — the centrifugal force — which also helped to raise the cargo, pulled by solar-driven electric engines out into space."

"Wow! Quite the contraption!"

"It worked. Tons of waste were hurled out toward distant star clusters, where eventually they'll incinerate, doing no harm in the meantime."

"So what Captain Kirk finds in the depths of unexplored space is barrels of spent plutonium floating toward distant galaxies?"

"Captain Kirk?" Lillian asked quizzically.

"The lead character in *Star Trek*."

"The one where nobody ever asked leave for the toilet."

"That's right," Vanessa said, and laughed. "A 60s thing, never mind."

"You can fill me in on the 60s another time," Lillian said with a smile.

"Sure, along with that dark-blue tie-dye you have on."

"My shirt? What's the matter with it?"

"Nothing," Vanessa said. "Except, for me, a tie-dye like that is something hippies used to make in the bathroom sink. A total relic in my day."

Lillian laughed.

"You never said why this was like Christmas shopping."

"No, and I forget now!"

She paused, then continued, "Oh, I remember. Because you drive and drive all over the place, then you can't find a parking spot, and when you finally do and get into the mall, you can't find what you're looking for after all."

"I hope this'll go better than that," Lillian said.

"We'll find them."

"It's been exciting enough, just moving through time, whether or not we do! Thrilling!" Vanessa said. "Though I know it's important we find them. Or, find their captives, I really mean."

"I understand," Lillian said.

"The last thing I would've imagined is travelling through time. I mean, you imagine it — and there's lots of movies and what-have-you — but you'd never dream of doing so in reality."

"Everyone travels through time throughout their lives," Lillian said. "But of course I know what you mean."

"Look there!" Vanessa said, leaning forward to point at some structures poking through the greenery.

Lillian slowed the craft nearly to a stop.

"That's what's left of Melbourne," she said. "My workshop was a few miles west of here. Downtown is straight ahead. We can set down and walk, I think."

"Okay," Vanessa said. "That looks like a hangar over there."

"It's an arena, I think. That'll be perfect, if it's empty inside."

They piloted the craft to the ground in front of the arena. It was heavily grown over with vegetation, but its entry doors at one end were gone, offering a spacious opening.

Lillian lifted the ship in a hover and brought them though the opening into the arena. She turned on the spotlights she had fixed to the bottom side of the fuselage.

"Perfect," she said. "Perfect." Then after a pause, "Look up there, Vanessa. Bats."

Vanessa gasped as she saw the ceiling was covered with brown bats, hanging upside-down asleep. The craft pulling in had not disturbed them, nor had the spotlights drawn their attention. The floor of the arena was barren, having no sunlight admitted.

"If there's that many bats in here, it's probably not being used by other animals. A perfect hiding spot."

"We'll have to run the ship through the car wash after, though,"

Vanessa said. "The floor here is crunchy thick with droppings."

Lillian smiled and said, "A minor inconvenience for the safety of the location."

She got up from her seat and opened the locker for her revolvers. She pulled the holsters around her waist, closing the buckle and tightening the straps around her thighs. When her own were ready, she fastened another pair around Vanessa's waist.

"But I haven't been trained with these guns!" Vanessa protested.

"I didn't know you as well then, when I said that before," Lillian replied. "Here's your training. Hold it out in front of you with both hands. Point the barrel toward what you want to shoot. Gently squeeze the trigger and hold tight. There's quite a blast. This button is the safety. You have to switch that off before they'll fire."

"Okay," Vanessa said. "I get the idea. I used to shoot smaller handguns. It's a popular pastime in Texas."

"Great," Lillian said. "So I won't be worried for you."

She handed Vanessa an armoured vest to put on, and fastened her own.

"They're so light!" Vanessa said.

"Aren't they?" Lillian said. "But they'll stop just about anything these guys'll have. Here's the helmet and visor. It's also armoured. Both are cooled or heated, depending on outside conditions."

"Hey! All we need are boot rockets, and we could audition for the Iron Man movie!"

"Seen it," Lillian said. "Wasn't that great."

"Still to come in my time," Vanessa said.

"I'm not a big vintage movie fan," Lillian said, "though I did go to an ancient cyborg-visions festival once. *Ghost in the Shell*, the original, was the best of that lot, though an instance where technology never advanced to meet science fiction. There were never any true cerebral cyborgs created."

"Too complicated?"

"A brain can't just be plugged into a borg body like a cigarette lighter."

Lillian clipped sheathed machetes to each of their gun-belts, then pulled out a pair of thin mylar pullovers, handing one to Vanessa.

"What are these for?" Vanessa said. "It doesn't look like rain."

"These are in case of a shower of bat droppings. We can leave them hanging outside the arena."

"Thanks. I don't want to be covered with muck before we start."

"Do you think you'll be able to shoot to kill, Vanessa? Our lives may depend on it."

"Not normally. But these guys will be an exception, I think."

"It's still unnerving, for an intelligent person."

"In my time, most of the great shocks — things that would paralyze peoples' psyches as a nation — were to do with killing. Often just one person, like President Kennedy or Martin Luther King. Sometimes lots of people, like the H-bomb, or flying the airplanes into the buildings in New York City. Do they still know about Kent State in your time?"

"Chilling," Lillian said.

8

"We look like a pair of riot policemen," Vanessa said as they came out into the sunshine.

"With no civil disobedience to quell," Lillian replied. "Nobody around at all, in fact."

"I love these little helmet radios. They're so clear, and we can speak so softly."

"Sexy outfit," Lillian said with a grin, noticing how the tailoring accented Vanessa's shapely torso.

"Thanks," Vanessa replied with a giggle. "Glad we have them. This is like a jungle. It is a jungle."

Lillian drew her machete.

"I hate to take the road more trodden, but we wouldn't have a chance through the raw chaparral. The road is barely passable as it is."

"Do you know where we're going?"

"We'll try to get to my place first. It'd be buried now, I think, for everything to be hidden so long. It must've been discovered in a dig or something. Anyway, I know it's in this general direction."

Lillian pointed to the northwest.

"See that hill, with the little rocky outcrop. My shop was right beside there."

"Your hill would have eroded over five thousand years!"

"I can see it has. But it's a distinctive shape, regardless, and it's all we have to go on at the moment," Lillian replied.

"Wouldn't your shop have been given to someone else when you died, or left the institute?"

"I don't know. I must've asked them to seal up my little corner. Once you were an established presence, you could ask for quite a bit. Others did as well, in their areas of study. In turn, we produced a great deal of useful stuff."

Lillian walked in front, cutting away brush as they went.

"I don't know about my death either, though I thought about it when I was building the craft. Moving in time opens the door on a lot of knowledge, but some things are spooky to find out about."

"And it can get mixed up. Like, if you died here — forgive me for saying — there'd be no record of that in your own time. Or if the villains had gotten us, you'd have died before your own birth."

"I choose to see all that as the same as moving through space. Born in New York, died in California. That it'd seem odd only superficially. The same moving in time."

"*Anastrophe,*" Vanessa said.

Lillian gave her a wide smile.

"Yes, giving emphasis by putting things out of order."

"These suits are amazing. It's quite hot outside now, but I'm perfectly comfortable."

"Great, isn't it? The suit is cooling you. They were developed for guerilla warfare."

"So people were still fighting in your day?"

"Not nearly so much as they were in yours. In my time, there isn't the wealth for it. Waging war is a luxury item for a nation. There are still evil, avaricious people, mind you. But instead of sending tanks and planes and missiles over enemy borders, warfare changed to infiltration — usually trying to steal supplies and technologies, rather than enlarge territories."

"All the hard-won territories of all the centuries are returned to nature now."

"I'm glad for that! — the vegetation here is wonderful! Just look at the flowers! There's willowherb, foxglove, and phlox. And over this way, red valerian and buttercup. Beautiful."

"You know your flora, Lillian! But, the handsome plants notwithstanding, this is heavy going!"

There was an irregular clearing adjacent to Lillian's rocky hilltop, in vicinity of an ancient radio tower.

"Keep to the edges here. We don't want to be seen."

Lillian had hardly finished her sentence when the air came alive with the sound of machine-gun fire.

Bullets ripped through the leaves and brush around and behind them. Vanessa was hit in the chest with two or three rounds, the impacts lifting her off her feet. She fell splayed into the foliage.

With the precision of her training, Lillian drew her pistol. It's laser sight, in sync with her enhanced eye, easily located the gun nest on the second tier of the concrete base of the tower. She detected two creatures there, targeting their foreheads in turn, and sending home a single blast to each. Both skulls were shattered.

Like a hardball heavy-hitting a watermelon, Lillian thought.

Two more creatures moved briskly around the second-level tier of the tower from its other side. As they came around the corner to the side she was facing, Lillian picked them off like moving targets at a carnival shooting gallery.

Geez, I hate this. But they definitely started it.

Aware that Vanessa was on the ground struck by gunfire, Lillian proceeded all the way around the tower, carefully surveying the area in infrared. If there were others anywhere on the tower, their body heat would reveal them.

None was apparent. Lillian decided the area was secure and hurried back to Vanessa.

As she approached, Vanessa was trying to lift herself to her feet.

"Are you okay?" Lillian said urgently.

She was still gasping for breath and couldn't answer. Lillian pulled off her gloves and helped her back to the ground.

She unzipped her armoured vest, pulling it open to inspect the skin underneath where she'd been hit.

"Three rounds, one square in the center of your chest and two more just above your breast to the left."

Lillian gently ran her hand over the wounded spots.

"You'll have some nasty bruises there, but nothing more."

"Really winded me," Vanessa whispered in a part-breath.

"You have a word for me?" Lillian said to draw Vanessa's mind from her injuries.

"Easy — *sockdolager*."

"You got me there!"

"To give someone a blow. Early American, obsolete," she said with a wheeze.

Lillian opened the pouch on her belt and pulled out a vial, pouring the contents on Vanessa's skin.

"Witch hazel," she said.

"I like the smell of witch hazel," Vanessa said, trying to smile.

9

When Vanessa was ready to proceed, Lillian again took the lead along the jungle trail.

"You okay?"

"Not too bad," Vanessa answered lightly.

"Are you sure?"

"My one bazoom is pretty sore."

"I bet it is," Lillian replied, and laughed.

Ahead of them to one side of the path was a caved-in area, as though the earthen ceiling of an underground cave had collapsed, creating a sinkhole about thirty feet deep.

"I think that's where we're going right there," Lillian said.

They came to the edge and Lillian scanned the pit below.

"There!" she said brightly, pointing to the remains of a steel doorway poking out of the mud at the bottom of the sinkhole.

"Yes, I see!" Vanessa answered.

"That's my old hangar door, all right."

"But how did they get the craft out?"

"One section of the mud is only camouflage, a façade," a strange voice said.

Lillian and Vanessa turned around with a tremendous start to find themselves facing one of the creatures.

Lillian quickly stepped back and drew a revolver from its holster, pointing it at his chest. Almost as quickly, the creature raised both arms in the air. Vanessa also drew a revolver, which she held at arms length, training it back and forth across the facing perimeter in front of the pit. There could be others hiding in the jungle.

"Come forth!" the first creature called.

Another alien came out of the jungle and crossed the clearing to stand just behind the first.

"There are only my servant and myself, and we are unarmed. My name is Agnash."

"Why have you come here?"

"To see you, Lillian Andarta," Agnash replied.

"And why unarmed and alone — if indeed you are — when lately in Vanessa's time you tried to destroy us?"

How we speak to mutants, Vanessa thought.

"You have every cause for suspicion."

"And you dragged away innocent people — to their deaths I bet!" Vanessa blurted out.

"That is also correct," Agnash said.

"So what do you expect us to think now?" Lillian said.

"In coming here I have committed myself to your superior intelligence and compassion," Agnash said, "in the belief you would not exterminate us in blind revenge, but that we would have the opportunity to explain ourselves and plead for your help."

"I don't trust him for a second," Vanessa said.

"You have no reason to trust us. Indeed, until this very morning I was committed to your destruction, in service of our larger cause in this time. But circumstances have changed, have further evolved, and I am now in need."

"Whichever way the wind blows to gratify your purposes, is it?" Vanessa said snidely.

"That is correct," Agnash responded.

"Well, at least he's candid," Lillian said.

"May we lower our hands?" Agnash asked.

"Okay, but keep your distance," Lillian answered.

"I would like to bring you to my home, where we can sit."

"Okay," Lillian said, "but don't be offended if I keep my pistol drawn."

10

"That is the story of my mission. Even this morning I blamed you for its failure and vowed revenge upon you."

The sun was beginning to set. The four had been talking for two hours. They'd originally been inside, but Vanessa suggested they go out. She didn't say so, but she couldn't tolerate the smell of Agnash and his companion.

"Lillian didn't have anything to do with it," Vanessa blurted out.

"I recognize that now," Agnash said.

"Sabotaging your plans — especially in this regard — would've been something quite beyond my power," Lillian added.

"We had no idea what was going on, especially why you'd try to kill us," Vanessa said.

"You would discover what we were doing and were equipped to oppose me. That threat had to be eliminated."

"How would she discover your plans?" Vanessa asked. "That doesn't make any sense."

She stood and faced Agnash to listen to his response.

"Perhaps not, but an effective military action takes all reasonable possibilities into account. If you discovered we were taking human organs and blood, you would have endeavoured to stop us. No other knowledge of our situation would have been in consideration."

"Well, you didn't do your homework about the bioregeneration procedure. We already knew it didn't work."

"I concede the extreme gravity of our need obscured my finer sensibilities."

"So what are you going to do now?"

"We have surrendered ourselves to your mercy. Or, I should say instead, your compassion."

"Covering our objections with a fat layer of humility," Vanessa said. "Ever the strategist."

"There is truth in what you say, Miss Vanessa. But my doing so is not an evil. My race is nearly extinct. How would you behave on behalf of your people in those circumstances?"

"With similar mercenary justice, I suppose," Vanessa muttered.

"While I was selected by our leaders for my ruthlessness, this was in the service of the preservation of the human race."

"In the corrupt form it has attained."

"That is irrelevant. This is the form and circumstance into which I was born. I did not ask for it. Moreover, having said that, you should understand our resentment of your biological privilege. What entitlement have you to a superior condition? Moreover, Cro-Magnon men might well find Ms. Andarta's mechanical parts as corrupt as you do our later condition of the species."

"Okay, I'll accept that," Vanessa said. "There but for the grace of the angels and all that."

"Let's get back to what he wants," Lillian said.

"To go back in time to a place where the few that survive here can live out their lives, to whatever that may amount."

"Why haven't you just gone?!"

"As you know Lillian, events progress only to their absolute outcome in time. It has occurred here that our efforts failed, and we are the last five living of our kind, after those killed on your arrival. It happened in this instantaneous present, as the amalgam of all events travelled to or from, or naturally lived by, the whole of all civilizations gone by."

Agnash, whose head had fallen as he spoke, looked up suddenly.

"Please forgive my lament," he added.

"Not at all," Lillian said.

"You didn't say why you haven't just gone," Vanessa said.

"The machine has been damaged," Agnash said. "I cannot reset a valid time signature."

"And?" Lillian said.

"And I want you — I want to ask you — if you would manually create a single signature for us to escape to the past."

"Where would you like to go?"

"To the American desert, in a primitive time. We can survive in the dry warmth and be refreshed sufficiently to live out a few more years. Here, now, there are too many infections to prey upon us, against which our bodies have little protection, but which your stronger immune systems easily destroy — the objective of our taking blood and tissues from the past to renew our own, as I know you understand. Where only semi-arid, there will be enough vegetation for our nourishment. I have an enthusiasm for botany, which will provide interest beyond the occupation of our food and shelter."

"Okay," Lillian said. "I'll do that for you."

"Wait a minute," Vanessa said quietly. "Those ancient Zuni petroglyphs that look like tall aliens! Could they be portraits of our buddies here?"

"Here I thought they were dreamscapes," Lillian said.

II

"Strange. The world is empty of people," Vanessa said.

"Except for you and me," Lillian replied with a smile. "Of course, the planet has been empty of people throughout most of its history."

Were there heavens and hells when the earth was empty? Were there gods and demi-gods, with only brutes and animals to rule?

They were walking through the jungle, back to the arena where their vehicle was parked.

"What shall we do?" Vanessa asked.

"For you and me? We have to keep going."

"What do you mean?"

"I mean, we just keep going. That's the only way I know how to say it."

Lillian smiled.

"Maybe I didn't understand the question," she added.

"I was only wondering," Vanessa clarified, "do we go home now, or is there something more that we should do here?"

"Oh, I see. Well, I don't want to stay in this time."

Arriving at the clearing in front of the arena, they sat on the ground in the sunshine.

"It's odd, but I feel the same urge as Agnash. To renew the species. In a better condition than them, mind you! Renewed to our kind. Or rather, your kind. I need too many spare parts." After a pause she added, "That's something we could do."

"What?" Vanessa asked.

"To bring healthy people here, from some earlier time."

"Why, yes! We'd be saving humanity! Cheating extinction!"

"I suppose," Lillian said with a smile. "But I wasn't thinking of that. In itself, there's nothing noble about saving humanity. Nothing at all. Species come and go. It's natural."

"But isn't this what the Great Goddess might've intended?"

"Possibly. By her time people were certainly liberating themselves. There'd been a big transformation building since about 500 B.C., with Shakyamuni, Confucius, and the Vedas. And in Greece. And Zoroaster in Persia a little later."

"But no liberations in one lifetime now, without any lifetimes available to live," Vanessa said.

"Not on this world, certainly. But we have a narrow view of sentient life, I think. The cosmos is vast."

"Wouldn't there still be a lot of people who'd want to resolve things here?"

"I don't know, I suppose so — I do know that, for deliverance, to realize her own Tara-nature, the White Goddess needs everyone over to her side of the mist bridge."

"The yogis said the same thing. But not just for her deliverance, for everyone's. That's why they'd come back time after time."

"The idea of that inseparability is subtle," Lillian said. "I'm a little surprised to hear you say it."

"I just read once that the entire audience has to applaud before the show's over," Vanessa added.

"Except possibly in Japan," Lillian said with a smile.

"One hand clapping will do," Vanessa answered, picking up the thread, and they laughed.

"Meanwhile, though, I value the journey," Lillian continued. "You just have to work down your attachments as you go, regarding your life activity with the same distance you regard your dreams — while being careful about what you do. Your actions in life greet you on the other side like a crowd of eager admirers."

"But what about the people you love, or if you have a child? Or if there were someone you'd been with a very, very long time?"

"You need to treat everyone the same way you'd treat that child, or your friend of the ages, I think."

"Whether one, two, or no hands clapping."

"That's right."

"We just keep going," Vanessa said.

"Yes," Lillian answered.

They both shrugged, raising their eyebrows.

"Whatever it is, wouldn't it be obvious if we went grabbing people? I don't want photos of us in all the tabloids as the 'alien abductors' ourselves."

"No, certainly not. But there are people in different times who surely wouldn't be missed, and who'd be happy for the relocation."

"Who are you thinking of?" Vanessa asked.

"I'm thinking of natural disasters — like Pompeii."

"Snatching people out at the last minute?"

"Yes, exactly."

"Okay, good deal! Let's go!"

"Hey! This seems quite a big thing to commence on such short consideration!" Lillian said.

"Yes," Vanessa said. "It is."

"Do you have a word come to mind?" Lillian asked, as much to give herself a moment to think.

"Um, for them I do, for those we rescue. *Thaumaturgy.*"

"Miracle working, certainly."

"Let's go," Vanessa said in a soft voice, reassuringly. "We'll have to find farmers and herders, though, who'll have a chance to survive here. From Pompeii, as you said, or maybe Troy, or Krakatoa.

Or maybe some drought-stricken ancient Yutes from America. It's just about limitless, really."

"Yes, quite! No shortage of disasters anyway. Still, it'll be quite hard for them, starting from scratch."

"Just know yourself, Vanessa, that hardship is the only way you have to work down your own past misdeeds. Be thankful for it. Thank your enemies as well, and mean it."

"Oh!" Vanessa added suddenly.

"What is it?" Lillian asked.

"Talking about dreams, and then about the ancients around the Mediterranean a minute ago, brought something to mind. Something from when I was very young."

"What's that?" Lillian asked.

"I'm a little reluctant to say."

Lillian just smiled, her face expectant.

"Do you think we could find England in the 1920s?"

"Sure. But why?"

"Well, I used to have dreams when I was little. Though, this is not to do with them having any immediate moment or not. These dreams were more like remembering. At least I believed it was a kind of remembering."

"Remembering a dream in your dream?"

"But a dream I never had."

"Yes, I understand. Like the myth writers."

"You're so sympathetic," Vanessa said, giving Lillian's hand a warm squeeze.

"So what's in England then?"

"Some others we can spare a few thousand years of ignominy. At a music hall there, in a seaside town."

Lillian suddenly noticed the words in rubbed ink on the back of Vanessa's hand.

"By the way," she said. "Who is 'Big Nose'?"

"I think that must be you, Lillian."